I0764565

Lucy Maud Montgomery

Short Stories, 1904

By

Lucy Maud Montgomery

Cover Artwork: goddessofchocolate

ISBN: 978-1-78139-241-6

© 2012 Oxford City Press, Oxford.

Contents

A Fortunate Mistake

"Oh, dear! oh, dear!" fretted Nan Wallace, twisting herself about uneasily on the sofa in her pretty room. "I never thought before that the days could be so long as they are now."

"Poor you!" said her sister Maude sympathetically. Maude was moving briskly about the room, putting it into the beautiful order that Mother insisted on. It was Nan's week to care for their room, but Nan had sprained her ankle three days ago and could do nothing but lie on the sofa ever since. And very tired of it, too, was wide-awake, active Nan.

"And the picnic this afternoon, too!" she sighed. "I've looked forward to it all summer. And it's a perfect day—and I've got to stay here and nurse this foot."

Nan looked vindictively at the bandaged member, while Maude leaned out of the window to pull a pink climbing rose. As she did so she nodded to someone in the village street below.

"Who is passing?" asked Nan.

"Florrie Hamilton."

"Is she going to the picnic?" asked Nan indifferently.

"No. She wasn't asked. Of course, I don't suppose she expected to be. She knows she isn't in our set. She must feel horribly out of place at school. A lot of the girls say it is ridiculous of her father to send her to Miss Braxton's private school—a factory overseer's daughter."

"She ought to have been asked to the picnic all the same," said Nan shortly. "She is in our class if she isn't in our set. Of course I don't suppose she would have enjoyed herself—or even gone at all, for that matter. She certainly doesn't push herself in among us. One would think she hadn't a tongue in her head."

"She is the best student in the class," admitted Maude, arranging her roses in a vase and putting them on the table at Nan's elbow. "But

Patty Morrison and Wilhelmina Patterson had the most to say about the invitations, and they wouldn't have her. There, Nannie dear, aren't those lovely? I'll leave them here to be company for you."

"I'm going to have more company than that," said Nan, thumping her pillow energetically. "I'm not going to mope here alone all the afternoon, with you off having a jolly time at the picnic. Write a little note for me to Florrie Hastings, will you? I'll do as much for you when you sprain your foot."

"What shall I put in it?" said Maude, rummaging out her portfolio obligingly.

"Oh, just ask her if she will come down and cheer a poor invalid up this afternoon. She'll come, I know. And she is such good company. Get Dickie to run right out and mail it."

"I do wonder if Florrie Hamilton will feel hurt over not being asked to the picnic," speculated Maude absently as she slipped her note into an envelope and addressed it.

Florrie Hamilton herself could best have answered that question as she walked along the street in the fresh morning sunshine. She did feel hurt—much more keenly than she would acknowledge even to herself. It was not that she cared about the picnic itself: as Nan Wallace had said, she would not have been likely to enjoy herself if she had gone among a crowd of girls many of whom looked down on her and ignored her. But to be left out when every other girl in the school was invited! Florrie's lip quivered as she thought of it.

"I'll get Father to let me to go to the public school after vacation," she murmured. "I hate going to Miss Braxton's."

Florrie was a newcomer in Winboro. Her father had recently come to take a position in the largest factory of the small town. For this reason Florrie was slighted at school by some of the ruder girls and severely left alone by most of the others. Some, it is true, tried at the start to be friends, but Florrie, too keenly sensitive to the atmosphere around her to respond, was believed to be decidedly dull and mopy. She retreated further and further into herself and was almost as solitary at Miss Braxton's as if she had been on a desert island.

"They don't like me because I am plainly dressed and because my father is not a wealthy man," thought Florrie bitterly. And there was enough truth in this in regard to many of Miss Braxton's girls to make a very uncomfortable state of affairs.

"Here's a letter for you, Flo," said her brother Jack at noon. "Got it at the office on my way home. Who is your swell correspondent?"

Florrie opened the dainty, perfumed note and read it with a face that, puzzled at first, suddenly grew radiant.

"Listen, Jack," she said excitedly.

"Dear Florrie:

> "Nan is confined to house, room, and sofa with a sprained foot. As she will be all alone this afternoon, won't you come down and spend it with her? She very much wants you to come—she is so lonesome and thinks you will be just the one to cheer her up.
>
> "Yours cordially,
> "Maude Wallace."

"Are you going?" asked Jack.

"Yes—I don't know—I'll think about it," said Florrie absently. Then she hurried upstairs to her room.

"Shall I go?" she thought. "Yes, I will. I dare say Nan has asked me just out of pity because I was not invited to the picnic. But even so it was sweet of her. I've always thought I would like those Wallace girls if I could get really acquainted with them. They've always been nice to me, too—I don't know why I am always so tongue-tied and stupid with them. But I'll go anyway."

That afternoon Mrs. Wallace came into Nan's room.

"Nan, dear, Florrie Hamilton is downstairs asking for you."

"Florrie—Hamilton?"

"Yes. She said something about a note you sent her this morning. Shall I ask her to come up?"

"Yes, of course," said Nan lamely. When her mother had gone out she fell back on her pillows and thought rapidly.

"Florrie Hamilton! Maude must have addressed that note to her by mistake. But she mustn't know it was a mistake—mustn't suspect it. Oh, dear! What shall I ever find to talk to her about? She is so quiet and shy."

Further reflections were cut short by Florrie's entrance. Nan held out her hand with a chummy smile.

"It's good of you to give your afternoon up to visiting a cranky invalid," she said heartily. "You don't know how lonesome I've been since Maude went away. Take off your hat and pick out the nicest chair you can find, and let's be comfy."

Somehow, Nan's frank greeting did away with Florrie's embarrassment and made her feel at home. She sat down in Maude's rocker, then, glancing over to a vase filled with roses, her eyes kindled with pleasure. Seeing this, Nan said, "Aren't they lovely? We Wallaces are very fond of our climbing roses. Our great-grandmother brought the roots out from England with her sixty years ago, and they grow nowhere else in this country."

"I know," said Florrie, with a smile. "I recognized them as soon as I came into the room. They are the same kind of roses as those which grow about Grandmother Hamilton's house in England. I used to love them so."

"In England! Were you ever in England?"

"Oh, yes," laughed Florrie. "And I've been in pretty nearly every other country upon earth—every one that a ship could get to, at least."

"Why, Florrie Hamilton! Are you in earnest?"

"Indeed, yes. Perhaps you don't know that our 'now-mother,' as Jack says sometimes, is Father's second wife. My own mother died when I was a baby, and my aunt, who had no children of her own, took me to bring up. Her husband was a sea-captain, and she always went on his sea-voyages with him. So I went too. I almost grew up on shipboard. We had delightful times. I never went to school. Auntie had been a teacher before her marriage, and she taught me. Two years ago, when I was fourteen, Father married again, and then he wanted me to go home to him and Jack and our new mother. So I did, although at first I was very sorry to leave Auntie and the dear old ship and all our lovely wanderings."

"Oh, tell me all about them," demanded Nan. "Why, Florrie Hamilton, to think you've never said a word about your wonderful experiences! I love to hear about foreign countries from people who have really been there. Please just talk—and I'll listen and ask questions."

Florrie did talk. I'm not sure whether she or Nan was the more surprised to find that she could talk so well and describe her travels so brightly and humorously. The afternoon passed quickly, and when Florrie went away at dusk, after a dainty tea served up in Nan's room, it was with a cordial invitation to come again soon.

"I've enjoyed your visit so much," said Nan sincerely. "I'm going down to see you as soon as I can walk. But don't wait for that. Let us be good, chummy friends without any ceremony."

When Florrie, with a light heart and a happy smile, had gone, came Maude, sunburned and glowing from her picnic.

"Such a nice time as we had!" she exclaimed. "Wasn't I sorry to think of you cooped up here! Did Florrie come?"

"One Florrie did. Maude, you addressed that note to Florrie Hamilton today instead of Florrie Hastings."

"Nan, surely not! I'm sure—"

"Yes, you did. And she came here. Was I not taken aback at first, Maude!"

"I was thinking about her when I addressed it, and I must have put her name down by mistake. I'm so sorry—"

"You needn't be. I haven't been entertained so charmingly for a long while. Why, Maude, she has travelled almost everywhere—and is so bright and witty when she thaws out. She didn't seem like the same girl at all. She is just perfectly lovely!"

"Well, I'm glad you had such a nice time together. Do you know, some of the girls were very much vexed because she wasn't asked to the picnic. They said that it was sheer rudeness not to ask her, and that it reflected on us all, even if Patty and Wilhelmina were responsible for it. I'm afraid we girls at Miss Braxton's have been getting snobbish, and some of us are beginning to find it out and be ashamed of it."

"Just wait until school opens," said Nan—vaguely enough, it would seem. But Maude understood.

However, they did not have to wait until school opened. Long before that time Winboro girlhood discovered that the Wallace girls were taking Florrie Hamilton into their lives. If the Wallace girls liked her, there must be something in the girl more than was at first thought—thus more than one of Miss Braxton's girls reasoned. And gradually the other girls found, as Nan had found, that Florrie was full of fun and an all-round good companion when drawn out of her diffidence. When Miss Braxton's school reopened Florrie was the class favourite. Between her and Nan Wallace a beautiful and helpful friendship had been formed which was to grow and deepen through their whole lives.

"And all because Maude in a fit of abstraction wrote 'Hamilton' for 'Hastings,'" said Nan to herself one day. But that is something Florrie Hamilton will never know.

An Unpremeditated Ceremony

Selwyn Grant sauntered in upon the assembled family at the homestead as if he were returning from an hour's absence instead of a western sojourn of ten years. Guided by the sound of voices on the still, pungent autumnal air, he went around to the door of the dining room which opened directly on the poppy walk in the garden.

Nobody noticed him for a moment and he stood in the doorway looking at them with a smile, wondering what was the reason of the festal air that hung about them all as visibly as a garment. His mother sat by the table, industriously polishing the best silver spoons, which, as he remembered, were only brought forth upon some great occasion. Her eyes were as bright, her form as erect, her nose—the Carston nose—as pronounced and aristocratic as of yore.

Selwyn saw little change in her. But was it possible that the tall, handsome young lady with the sleek brown pompadour and a nose unmistakably and plebeianly Grant, who sat by the window doing something to a heap of lace and organdy in her lap, was the little curly-headed, sunburned sister of thirteen whom he remembered? The young man leaning against the sideboard must be Leo, of course; a fine-looking, broad-shouldered young fellow who made Selwyn think suddenly that he must be growing old. And there was the little, thin, grey father in the corner, peering at his newspaper with nearsighted eyes. Selwyn's heart gave a bound at the sight of him which not even his mother had caused. Dear old Dad! The years had been kind to him.

Mrs. Grant held up a glistening spoon and surveyed it complacently. "There, I think that is bright enough even to suit Margaret Graham. I shall take over the whole two dozen teas and one dozen desserts. I wish, Bertha, that you would tie a red cord around each of the handles for me. The Carmody spoons are the same pattern and I shall always be convinced that Mrs. Carmody carried off two of ours the time that

Jenny Graham was married. I don't mean to take any more risks. And, Father——"

Something made the mother look around, and she saw her first-born!

When the commotion was over Selwyn asked why the family spoons were being rubbed up.

"For the wedding, of course," said Mrs. Grant, polishing her gold-bowed spectacles and deciding that there was no more time for tears and sentiment just then. "And there, they're not half done—and we'll have to dress in another hour. Bertha is no earthly use—she is so taken up with her bridesmaid finery."

"Wedding? Whose wedding?" demanded Selwyn, in bewilderment.

"Why, Leo's, of course. Leo is to be married tonight. Didn't you get your invitation? Wasn't that what brought you home?"

"Hand me a chair, quick," implored Selwyn. "Leo, are *you* going to commit matrimony in this headlong fashion? Are you sure you're grown up?"

"Six feet is a pretty good imitation of it, isn't it?" grinned Leo. "Brace up, old fellow. It's not so bad as it might be. She's quite a respectable girl. We wrote you all about it three weeks ago and broke the news as gently as possible."

"I left for the East a month ago and have been wandering around preying on old college chums ever since. Haven't seen a letter. There, I'm better now. No, you needn't fan me, Sis. Well, no family can get through the world without its seasons of tribulations. Who is the party of the second part, little brother?"

"Alice Graham," replied Mrs. Grant, who had a habit of speaking for her children, none of whom had the Carston nose.

"Alice Graham! That child!" exclaimed Selwyn in astonishment.

Leo roared. "Come, come, Sel, perhaps we're not very progressive here in Croyden, but we don't actually stand still. Girls are apt to stretch out some between ten and twenty, you know. You old bachelors think nobody ever grows up. Why, Sel, you're grey around your temples."

"Too well I know it, but a man's own brother shouldn't be the first to cast such things up to him. I'll admit, since I come to think of it, that Alice has probably grown bigger. Is she any better-looking than she used to be?"

"Alice is a charming girl," said Mrs. Grant impressively. "She is a beauty and she is also sweet and sensible, which beauties are not always. We are all very much pleased with Leo's choice. But we have really no more time to spare just now. The wedding is at seven o'clock and it is four already."

"Is there anybody you can send to the station for my luggage?" asked Selwyn. "Luckily I have a new suit, otherwise I shouldn't have the face to go."

"Well, I must be off," said Mrs. Grant. "Father, take Selwyn away so that I shan't be tempted to waste time talking to him."

In the library father and son looked at each other affectionately.

"Dad, it's a blessing to see you just the same. I'm a little dizzy with all these changes. Bertha grown up and Leo within an inch of being married! To Alice Graham at that, whom I can't think of yet as anything else than the long-legged, black-eyed imp of mischief she was when a kiddy. To tell you the truth, Dad, I don't feel in a mood for going to a wedding at Wish-ton-wish tonight. I'm sure you don't either. You've always hated fusses. Can't we shirk it?"

They smiled at each other with chummy remembrance of many a family festival they had "shirked" together in the old days. But Mr. Grant shook his head. "Not this time, sonny. There are some things a decent man can't shirk and one of them is his own boy's wedding. It's a nuisance, but I must go through with it. You'll understand how it is when you're a family man yourself. By the way, why aren't you a family man by this time? Why haven't I been put to the bother and inconvenience of attending your wedding before now, son?"

Selwyn laughed, with a little vibrant note of bitterness in the laughter, which the father's quick ears detected. "I've been too busy with law books, Dad, to find me a wife."

Mr. Grant shook his bushy grey head. "That's not the real reason, son. The world has a wife for every man; if he hasn't found her by the time he's thirty-five, there's some real reason for it. Well, I don't want to pry into yours, but I hope it's a sound one and not a mean, sneaking, selfish sort of reason. Perhaps you'll choose a Madam Selwyn some day yet. In case you should I'm going to give you a small bit of good advice. Your mother—now, she's a splendid woman, Selwyn, a splendid woman. She can't be matched as a housekeeper and she has improved my finances until I don't know them when I meet them. She's been a good wife and a good mother. If I were a young man I'd court her and marry her over again, that I would. But, son, when *you* pick a wife pick one with a nice little commonplace nose, not a family nose. Never marry a woman with a family nose, son."

A woman with a family nose came into the library at this juncture and beamed maternally upon them both. "There's a bite for you in the dining room. After you've eaten it you must dress. Mind you brush your hair well down, Father. The green room is ready for you, Selwyn. Tomorrow I'll have a good talk with you, but tonight I'll be too busy to remember you're around. How are we all going to get over to Wish-ton-wish? Leo and Bertha are going in the pony carriage. It won't hold a third passenger. You'll have to squeeze in with Father and me in the buggy, Selwyn."

"By no means," replied Selwyn briskly. "I'll walk over to Wish-ton-wish. Ifs only half a mile across lots. I suppose the old way is still open?"

"It ought to be," answered Mr. Grant drily; "Leo has kept it well trodden. If you've forgotten how it runs he can tell you."

"I haven't forgotten," said Selwyn, a little brusquely. He had his own reasons for remembering the wood path. Leo had not been the first Grant to go courting to Wish-ton-wish.

When he started, the moon was rising round and red and hazy in an eastern hill-gap. The autumn air was mild and spicy. Long shadows stretched across the fields on his right and silvery mosaics patterned the floor of the old beechwood lane. Selwyn walked slowly. He was thinking of Esme Graham or, rather, of the girl who had been Esme Graham, and wondering if he would see her at the wedding. It was probable, and he did not want to see her. In spite of ten years' effort, he did not think he could yet look upon Tom St. Clair's wife with the proper calm indifference. At the best, it would taint his own memory of her; he would never again be able to think of her as Esme Graham but only as Esme St. Clair.

The Grahams had come to Wish-ton-wish eleven years before. There was a big family of girls of whom the tall, brown-haired Esme was the oldest. There was one summer during which Selwyn Grant had haunted Wish-ton-wish, the merry comrade of the younger girls, the boyishly, silently devoted lover of Esme. Tom St. Clair had always been there too, in his right as second cousin, Selwyn had supposed. One day he found out that Tom and Esme had been engaged ever since she was sixteen; one of her sisters told him. That had been all. He had gone away soon after, and some time later a letter from home made casual mention of Tom St. Clair's marriage.

He narrowly missed being late for the wedding ceremony. The bridal party entered the parlour at Wish-ton-wish at the same moment as he slipped in by another door. Selwyn almost whistled with amazement at sight of the bride. *That* Alice Graham, that tall, stately, blushing young woman, with her masses of dead-black hair, frosted over by the film of wedding veil! Could that be the scrawny little tomboy of ten years ago? She looked not unlike Esme, with that subtle family resemblance that is quite independent of feature and colouring.

Where was Esme? Selwyn cast his eyes furtively over the assembled guests while the minister read the marriage ceremony. He recognized several of the Graham girls but he did not see Esme, although Tom St. Clair, stout and florid and prosperous-looking, was standing on a chair in a faraway corner, peering over the heads of the women.

After the turmoil of handshakings and congratulations, Selwyn fled to the cool, still outdoors, where the rosy glow of Chinese lanterns mingled with the waves of moonshine to make fairyland. And there he met her, as she came out of the house by a side door, a tall, slender woman in some glistening, clinging garment, with white flowers shining like stars in the coils of her brown hair. In the soft glow she looked even more beautiful than in the days of her girlhood, and Selwyn's heart throbbed dangerously at sight of her.

"Esme!" he said involuntarily.

She started, and he had an idea that she changed colour, although it was too dim to be sure. "Selwyn!" she exclaimed, putting out her hands. "Why, Selwyn Grant! Is it really you? Or are you such stuff as dreams are made of? I did not know you were here. I did not know you were home."

He caught her hands and held them tightly, drawing her a little closer to him, forgetting that she was Tom St. Clair's wife, remembering only that she was the woman to whom he had given all his love and life's devotion, to the entire beggaring of his heart.

"I reached home only four hours ago, and was haled straightway here to Leo's wedding. I'm dizzy, Esme. I can't adjust my old conceptions to this new state of affairs all at once. It seems ridiculous to think that Leo and Alice are married. I'm sure they can't be really grown up."

Esme laughed as she drew away her hands. "We are all ten years older," she said lightly.

"Not you. You are more beautiful than ever, Esme. That sunflower compliment is permissible in an old friend, isn't it?"

"This mellow glow is kinder to me than sunlight now. I am thirty, you know, Selwyn."

"And I have some grey hairs," he confessed. "I knew I had them but I had a sneaking hope that other folks didn't until Leo destroyed it today. These young brothers and sisters who won't stay children are nuisances. You'll be telling me next thing that 'Baby' is grown up."

"'Baby' is eighteen and has a beau," laughed Esme. "And I give you fair warning that she insists on being called Laura now. Do you want to come for a walk with me—down under the beeches to the old lane gate? I came out to see if the fresh air would do my bit of a headache good. I shall have to help with the supper later on."

They went slowly across the lawn and turned into a dim, moonlight lane beyond, their old favourite ramble. Selwyn felt like a man in a dream, a pleasant dream from which he dreads to awaken. The voices and laughter echoing out from the house died away behind them and the great silence of the night fell about them as they came to the old gate, beyond which was a range of shining, moonlight-misted fields.

For a little while neither of them spoke. The woman looked out across the white spaces and the man watched the glimmering curve of her neck and the soft darkness of her rich hair. How virginal, how sacred, she looked! The thought of Tom St. Clair was a sacrilege.

"It's nice to see you again, Selwyn," said Esme frankly at last. "There are so few of our old set left, and so many of the babies grown up. Sometimes I don't know my own world, it has changed so. It's an uncomfortable feeling. You give me a pleasant sensation of really belonging here. I'd be lonesome tonight if I dared. I'm going to miss Alice so much. There will be only Mother and Baby and I left now. Our family circle has dwindled woefully."

"Mother and Baby and you!" Selwyn felt his head whirling again. "Why, where is Tom?"

He felt that it was an idiotic question, but it slipped from his tongue before he could catch it. Esme turned her head and looked at him wonderingly. He knew that in the sunlight her eyes were as mistily blue as early meadow violets, but here they looked dark and unfathomably tender.

"Tom?" she said perplexedly. "Do you mean Tom St. Clair? He is here, of course, he and his wife. Didn't you see her? That pretty woman in pale pink, Lil Meredith. Why, you used to know Lil, didn't you? One of the Uxbridge Merediths?"

To the day of his death Selwyn Grant will firmly believe that if he had not clutched fast hold of the top bar of the gate he would have tumbled down on the moss under the beeches in speechless astonishment. All the surprises of that surprising evening were as nothing to this. He had a swift conviction that there were no words in the English language that could fully express his feelings and that it would be a waste of time to try to find any. Therefore he laid hold of the first baldly commonplace ones that came handy and said tamely, "I thought you were married to Tom."

"You—thought—I—was—married—to—Tom!" repeated Esme slowly. "And have you thought *that* all these years, Selwyn Grant?"

"Yes, I have. Is it any wonder? You were engaged to Tom when I went away, Jenny told me you were. And a year later Bertha wrote me a letter in which she made some reference to Tom's marriage. She didn't say to *whom*, but hadn't I the right to suppose it was to you?"

"Oh!" The word was partly a sigh and partly a little cry of long-concealed, long-denied pain. "It's been all a funny misunderstanding. Tom and I *were* engaged once—a boy-and-girl affair in the beginning. Then we both found out that we had made a mistake—that what we had thought was love was merely the affection of good comrades. We broke our engagement shortly before you went away. All the older girls knew it was broken but I suppose nobody mentioned the matter to Jen. She was such a child, we never thought about her. And you've thought I was Tom's wife all this time? It's—funny."

"Funny. You mean tragic! Look here, Esme, I'm not going to risk any more misunderstanding. There's nothing for it but plain talk when matters get to such a state as this. I love you—and I've loved you ever since I met you. I went away because I could not stay here and see you married to another man. I've stayed away for the same reason. Esme, is it too late? Did you ever care anything for me?"

"Yes, I did," she said slowly.

"Do you care still?" he asked.

She hid her face against his shoulder. "Yes," she whispered.

"Then we'll go back to the house and be married," he said joyfully.

Esme broke away and stared at him. "Married!"

"Yes, married. We've wasted ten years and we're not going to waste another minute. We're *not*, I say."

"Selwyn! It's impossible."

"I have expurgated that word from my dictionary. It's the very simplest thing when you look at it in an unprejudiced way. Here is a ready-made wedding and decorations and assembled guests, a minister on the spot and a state where no licence is required. You have a very pretty new dress on and you love me. I have a plain gold ring on my little finger that will fit you. Aren't all the conditions fulfilled? Where is the sense of waiting and having another family upheaval in a few weeks' time?"

"I understand why you have made such a success of the law," said Esme, "but—"

"There are no buts. Come with me, Esme. I'm going to hunt up your mother and mine and talk to them."

Half an hour later an astonishing whisper went circulating among the guests. Before they could grasp its significance Tom St. Clair and Jen's husband, broadly smiling, were hustling scattered folk into the parlour again and making clear a passage in the hall. The minister came in with his blue book, and then Selwyn Grant and Esme Graham walked in hand in hand.

When the second ceremony was over, Mr. Grant shook his son's hand vigorously. "There's no need to wish you happiness, son; you've got it. And you've made one fuss and bother do for both weddings, that's what I call genius. And"—this in a careful whisper, while Esme was temporarily obliterated in Mrs. Grant's capacious embrace—"she's got the right sort of a nose. But your mother is a grand woman, son, a grand woman."

At the Bay Shore Farm

The Newburys were agog with excitement over the Governor's picnic. As they talked it over on the verandah at sunset, they felt that life could not be worth living to those unfortunate people who had not been invited to it. Not that there were many of the latter in Claymont, for it was the Governor's native village, and the Claymonters were getting up the picnic for him during his political visit to the city fifteen miles away.

Each of the Newburys had a special reason for wishing to attend the Governor's picnic. Ralph and Elliott wanted to see the Governor himself. He was a pet hero of theirs. Had he not once been a Claymont lad just like themselves? Had he not risen to the highest office in the state by dint of sheer hard work and persistency? Had he not won a national reputation by his prompt and decisive measures during the big strike at Campden? And was he not a man, personally and politically, whom any boy might be proud to imitate? Yes, to all of these questions. Hence to the Newbury boys the interest of the picnic centred in the Governor.

"I shall feel two inches taller just to get a look at him," said Ralph enthusiastically.

"He isn't much to look at," said Frances, rather patronizingly. "I saw him once at Campden—he came to the school when his daughter was graduated. He is bald and fat. Oh, of course, he is famous and all that! But I want to go to the picnic to see Sara Beaumont. She's to be there with the Chandlers from Campden, and Mary Spearman, who knows her by sight, is going to point her out to me. I suppose it would be too much to expect to be introduced to her. I shall probably have to content myself with just looking at her."

Ralph resented hearing the Governor called bald and fat. Somehow it seemed as if his hero were being reduced to the level of common clay.

"That's like a girl," he said loftily; "thinking more about a woman who writes books than about a man like the Governor!"

"I'd rather see Sara Beaumont than forty governors," retorted Frances. "Why, she's famous—and her books are perfect! If I could ever hope to write anything like them! It's been the dream of my life just to see her ever since I read *The Story of Idlewild.* And now to think that it is to be fulfilled! It seems too good to be true that tomorrow—tomorrow, Newburys,—I shall see Sara Beaumont!"

"Well," said Cecilia gently—Cecilia was always gentle even in her enthusiasm—"I shall like to see the Governor and Sara Beaumont too. But I'm going to the picnic more for the sake of seeing Nan Harris than anything else. It's three years since she went away, you know, and I've never had another chum whom I love so dearly. I'm just looking forward to meeting her and talking over all our dear, good old times. I do wonder if she has changed much. But I am sure I shall know her."

"By her red hair and her freckles?" questioned Elliott teasingly. "They'll be the same as ever, I'll be bound."

Cecilia flushed and looked as angry as she could—which isn't saying much, after all. She didn't mind when Elliott teased her about her pug nose and her big mouth, but it always hurt her when he made fun of Nan.

Nan's family had once lived across the street from the Newburys. Nan and Cecilia had been playmates all through childhood, but when both girls were fourteen the Harrises had moved out west. Cecilia had never seen Nan since. But now the latter had come east for a visit, and was with her relatives in Campden. She was to be at the picnic, and Cecilia's cup of delight brimmed over.

Mrs. Newbury came briskly into the middle of their sunset plans. She had been down to the post office, and she carried an open letter in her hand.

"Mother," said Frances, straightening up anxiously, "you have a pitying expression on your face. Which of us is it for—speak out—don't keep us in suspense. Has Mary Spearman told you that Sara Beaumont isn't going to be at the picnic?"

"Or that the Governor isn't going to be there?"

"Or that Nan Harris isn't coming?"

"Or that something's happened to put off the affair altogether?" cried Ralph and Cecilia and Elliott all at once.

Mrs. Newbury laughed. "No, it's none of those things. And I don't know just whom I do pity, but it is one of you girls. This is a letter from Grandmother Newbury. Tomorrow is her birthday, and she wants either Frances or Cecilia to go out to Ashland on the early morning train and spend the day at the Bay Shore Farm."

There was silence on the verandah of the Newburys for the space of ten seconds. Then Frances burst out with: "Mother, you know neither of us can go tomorrow. If it were any other day! But the day of the picnic!"

"I'm sorry, but one of you must go," said Mrs. Newbury firmly. "Your father said so when I called at the store to show him the letter. Grandmother Newbury would be very much hurt and displeased if her invitation were disregarded—you know that. But we leave it to yourselves to decide which one shall go."

"Don't do that," implored Frances miserably. "Pick one of us yourself—pull straws—anything to shorten the agony."

"No; you must settle it for yourselves," said Mrs. Newbury. But in spite of herself she looked at Cecilia. Cecilia was apt to be looked at, someway, when things were to be given up. Mostly it was Cecilia who gave them up. The family had come to expect it of her; they all said that Cecilia was very unselfish.

Cecilia knew that her mother looked at her, but did not turn her face. She couldn't, just then; she looked away out over the hills and tried to swallow something that came up in her throat.

"Glad I'm not a girl," said Ralph, when Mrs. Newbury had gone into the house. "Whew! Nothing could induce me to give up that picnic—not if a dozen Grandmother Newburys were offended. Where's your sparkle gone now, Fran?"

"It's too bad of Grandmother Newbury," declared Frances angrily.

"Oh, Fran, she didn't know about the picnic," said Cecilia—but still without turning round.

"Well, she needn't always be so annoyed if we don't go when we are invited. Another day would do just as well," said Frances shortly. Something in her voice sounded choked too. She rose and walked to the other end of the verandah, where she stood and scowled down the road; Ralph and Elliott, feeling uncomfortable, went away.

The verandah was very still for a little while. The sun had quite set, and it was growing dark when Frances came back to the steps.

"Well, what are you going to do about it?" she said shortly. "Which of us is to go to the Bay Shore?"

"I suppose I had better go," said Cecilia slowly—very slowly indeed.

Frances kicked her slippered toe against the fern *jardinière.*

"You may see Nan Harris somewhere else before she goes back," she said consolingly.

"Yes, I may," said Cecilia. She knew quite well that she would not. Nan would return to Campden on the special train, and she was going back west in three days.

It was hard to give the picnic up, but Cecilia was used to giving things up. Nobody ever expected Frances to give things up; she was so brilliant and popular that the good things of life came her way naturally. It never seemed to matter so much about quiet Cecilia.

Cecilia cried herself to sleep that night. She felt that it was horribly selfish of her to do so, but she couldn't help it. She awoke in the morning with a confused idea that it was very late. Why hadn't Mary called her, as she had been told to do?

Through the open door between her room and Frances's she could see that the latter's bed was empty. Then she saw a little note, addressed to her, pinned on the pillow.

Dear Saint Cecilia [it ran], when you read this I shall be on the train to Ashland to spend the day with Grandmother Newbury. You've been giving up things so often and so long that I suppose you think you have a monopoly of it; but you see you haven't. I didn't tell you this last night because I hadn't quite made up my mind. But after you went upstairs, I fought it out to a finish and came to a decision. Sara Beaumont would keep, but Nan Harris wouldn't, so you must go to the picnic. I told Mary to call me instead of you this morning, and now I'm off. You needn't spoil your fun pitying me. Now that the wrench is over, I feel a most delightful glow of virtuous satisfaction!

Fran.

If by running after Frances Cecilia could have brought her back, Cecilia would have run. But a glance at her watch told her that Frances must already be halfway to Ashland. So she could only accept the situation.

"Well, anyway," she thought, "I'll get Mary to point Sara Beaumont out to me, and I'll store up a description of her in my mind to tell Fran tonight. I must remember to take notice of the colour of her eyes. Fran has always been exercised about that."

It was mid-forenoon when Frances arrived at Ashland station. Grandmother Newbury's man, Hiram, was waiting for her with the pony carriage, and Frances heartily enjoyed the three-mile drive to the Bay Shore Farm.

Grandmother Newbury came to the door to meet her granddaughter. She was a tall, handsome old lady with piercing black eyes and thick white hair. There was no savour of the traditional grandmother of caps and knitting about her. She was like a stately old princess and, much as her grandchildren admired her, they were decidedly in awe of her.

"So it is Frances," she said, bending her head graciously that Frances might kiss her still rosy cheek. "I expected it would be Cecilia. I heard after I had written you that there was to be a gubernatorial picnic in Claymont today, so I was quite sure it would be Cecilia. Why isn't it Cecilia?"

Frances flushed a little. There was a meaning tone in Grandmother Newbury's voice.

"Cecilia was very anxious to go to the picnic today to see an old friend of hers," she answered. "She was willing to come here, but you know, Grandmother, that Cecilia is always willing to do the things somebody else ought to do, so I decided I would stand on my rights as 'Miss Newbury' for once and come to the Bay Shore."

Grandmother Newbury smiled. She understood. Frances had always been her favourite granddaughter, but she had never been blind, clear-sighted old lady that she was, to the little leaven of easy-going selfishness in the girl's nature. She was pleased to see that Frances had conquered it this time.

"I'm glad it is you who have come—principally because you are cleverer than Cecilia," she said brusquely. "Or at least you are the better talker. And I want a clever girl and a good talker to help me entertain a guest today. She's clever herself, and she likes young girls. She is a particular friend of your Uncle Robert's family down south, and that is why I have asked her to spend a few days with me. You'll like her."

Here Grandmother Newbury led Frances into the sitting-room.

"Mrs. Kennedy, this is my granddaughter, Frances Newbury. I told you about her and her ambitions last night. You see, Frances, we have talked you over."

Mrs. Kennedy was a much younger woman than Grandmother Newbury. She was certainly no more than fifty and, in spite of her grey hair, looked almost girlish, so bright were her dark eyes, so clear-cut and fresh her delicate face, and so smart her general appearance.

Frances, although not given to sudden likings, took one for Mrs. Kennedy. She thought she had never seen so charming a face.

She found herself enjoying the day immensely. In fact, she forgot the Governor's picnic and Sara Beaumont altogether. Mrs. Kennedy proved to be a delightful companion. She had travelled extensively and was an excellent *raconteur*. She had seen much of men and women and crystallized her experiences into sparkling little sentences and epigrams which made Frances feel as if she were listening to one of the witty people in clever books. But under all her sparkling wit there was a strongly felt undercurrent of true womanly sympathy and kind-heartedness which won affection as speedily as her brilliance won admiration. Frances listened and laughed and enjoyed. Once she found time to think that she would have missed a great deal if she had not come to Bay Shore Farm that day. Surely talking to a woman like Mrs. Kennedy was better than looking at Sara Beaumont from a distance.

"I've been 'rewarded' in the most approved storybook style," she thought with amusement.

In the afternoon, Grandmother Newbury packed Mrs. Kennedy and Frances off for a walk.

"The old woman wants to have her regular nap," she told them. "Frances, take Mrs. Kennedy to the fern walk and show her the famous 'Newbury Bubble' among the rocks. I want to be rid of you both until tea-time."

Frances and Mrs. Kennedy went to the fern walk and the beautiful "Bubble"—a clear, round spring of amber-hued water set down in a cup of rock overhung with ferns and beeches. It was a spot Frances had always loved. She found herself talking freely to Mrs. Kennedy of her hopes and plans. The older woman drew the girl out with tactful sympathy until she found that Frances's dearest ambition was some day to be a writer of books like Sara Beaumont.

"Not that I expect ever to write books like hers," she said hurriedly, "and I know it must be a long while before I can write anything worth while at all. But do you think—if I try hard and work hard—that I might do something in this line some day?"

"I think so," said Mrs. Kennedy, smiling, "if, as you say, you are willing to work hard and study hard. There will be a great deal of both and many disappointments. Sara Beaumont herself had a hard time at first—and for a very long first too. Her family was poor, you know, and Sara earned enough money to send away her first manuscripts by making a pot of jelly for a neighbour. The manuscripts came back, and Sara made more jelly and wrote more stories. Still they came back.

Once she thought she had better give up writing stories and stick to the jelly alone. There did seem some little demand for the one and none at all for the other. But she determined to keep on until she either succeeded or proved to her own satisfaction that she could make better jelly than stories. And you see she did succeed. But it means perseverance and patience and much hard work. Prepare yourself for that, Frances, and one day you will win your place. Then you will look back to the 'Newbury Bubble,' and you will tell me what a good prophetess I was."

They talked longer—an earnest, helpful talk that went far to inspire Frances's hazy ambition with a definite purpose. She understood that she must not write merely to win fame for herself or even for the higher motive of pure pleasure in her work. She must aim, however humbly, to help her readers to higher planes of thought and endeavour. Then and only then would it be worth while.

"Mrs. Kennedy is going to drive you to the station," said Grandmother Newbury after tea. "I am much obliged to you, Frances, for giving up the picnic today and coming to the Bay Shore to gratify an old woman's inconvenient whim. But I shall not burden you with too much gratitude, for I think you have enjoyed yourself."

"Indeed, I have," said Frances heartily. Then she added with a laugh, "I think I would feel much more meritorious if it had not been so pleasant. It has robbed me of all the self-sacrificing complacency I felt this morning. You see, I wanted to go to that picnic to see Sara Beaumont, and I felt quite like a martyr at giving it up."

Grandmother Newbury's eyes twinkled. "You would have been beautifully disappointed had you gone. Sara Beaumont was not there. Mrs. Kennedy, I see you haven't told our secret. Frances, my dear, let me introduce you two over again. This lady is Mrs. Sara Beaumont Kennedy, the writer of *The Story of Idlewild* and all those other books you so much admire."

The Newburys were sitting on the verandah at dusk, too tired and too happy to talk. Ralph and Elliott had seen the Governor; more than that, they had been introduced to him, and he had shaken hands with them both and told them that their father and he had been chums when just their size. And Cecilia had spent a whole day with Nan Harris, who had not changed at all except to grow taller. But there was one little cloud on her content.

"I wanted to see Sara Beaumont to tell Frances about her, but I couldn't get a glimpse of her. I don't even know if she was there."

"There comes Fran up the station road now," said Ralph. "My eyes, hasn't she a step!"

Frances came smiling over the lawn and up the steps.

"So you are all home safe," she said gaily. "I hope you feasted your eyes on your beloved Governor, boys. I can tell that Cecilia forgathered with Nan by the beatific look on her face."

"Oh, Fran, it was lovely!" cried Cecilia. "But I felt so sorry—why didn't you let me go to Ashland? It was too bad you missed it—and Sara Beaumont."

"Sara Beaumont was at the Bay Shore Farm," said Frances. "I'll tell you all about it when I get my breath—I've been breathless ever since Grandmother Newbury told me of it. There's only one drawback to my supreme bliss—the remembrance of how complacently self-sacrificing I felt this morning. It humiliates me wholesomely to remember it!"

Elizabeth's Child

The Ingelows, of Ingelow Grange, were not a marrying family. Only one of them, Elizabeth, had married, and perhaps it was her "poor match" that discouraged the others. At any rate, Ellen and Charlotte and George Ingelow at the Grange were single, and so was Paul down at Greenwood Farm.

It was seventeen years since Elizabeth had married James Sheldon in the face of the most decided opposition on the part of her family. Sheldon was a handsome, shiftless ne'er-do-well, without any violent bad habits, but also "without any backbone," as the Ingelows declared. "There is sometimes hope of a man who is actively bad," Charlotte Ingelow had said sententiously, "but who ever heard of reforming a jellyfish?"

Elizabeth and her husband had gone west and settled on a prairie farm in Manitoba. She had never been home since. Perhaps her pride kept her away, for she had the Ingelow share of that, and she soon discovered that her family's estimate of James Sheldon had been the true one. There was no active resentment on either side, and once in a long while letters were exchanged. Still, ever since her marriage, Elizabeth had been practically an outsider and an alien. As the years came and went the Ingelows at home remembered only at long intervals that they had a sister on the western prairies.

One of these remembrances came to Charlotte Ingelow on a spring afternoon when the great orchards about the Grange were pink and white with apple and cherry blossoms, and over every hill and field was a delicate, flower-starred green. A soft breeze was blowing loose petals from the August Sweeting through the open door of the wide hall when Charlotte came through it. Ellen and George were standing on the steps outside.

"This kind of a day always makes me think of Elizabeth," said Charlotte dreamily. "It was in apple-blossom time she went away." The Ingelows always spoke of Elizabeth's going away, never of her marrying.

"Seventeen years ago," said Ellen. "Why, Elizabeth's oldest child must be quite a young woman now! I—I—" a sudden idea swept over and left her a little breathless. "I would really like to see her."

"Then why don't you write and ask her to come east and visit us?" asked George, who did not often speak, but who always spoke to some purpose when he did.

Ellen and Charlotte looked at each other. "I would like to see Elizabeth's child," repeated Ellen firmly.

"Do you think she would come?" asked Charlotte. "You know when James Sheldon died five years ago, we wrote to Elizabeth and asked her to come home and live with us, and she seemed almost resentful in the letter she wrote back. I've never said so before, but I've often thought it."

"Yes, she did," said Ellen, who had often thought so too, but never said so.

"Elizabeth was always very independent," remarked George. "Perhaps she thought your letter savoured of charity or pity. No Ingelow would endure that."

"At any rate, you know she refused to come, even for a visit. She said she could not leave the farm. She may refuse to let her child come."

"It won't do any harm to ask her," said George.

In the end, Charlotte wrote to Elizabeth and asked her to let her daughter visit the old homestead. The letter was written and mailed in much perplexity and distrust when once the glow of momentary enthusiasm in the new idea had passed.

"What if Elizabeth's child is like her father?" queried Charlotte in a half-whisper.

"Let us hope she won't be!" cried Ellen fervently. Indeed, she felt that a feminine edition of James Sheldon would be more than she could endure.

"She may not like us, or our ways," sighed Charlotte. "We don't know how she has been brought up. She will seem like a stranger after all. I really long to see Elizabeth's child, but I can't help fearing we have done a rash thing, Ellen."

"Perhaps she may not come," suggested Ellen, wondering whether she hoped it or feared it.

But Worth Sheldon did come. Elizabeth wrote back a prompt acceptance, with no trace of the proud bitterness that had permeated her answer to the former invitation. The Ingelows at the Grange were thrown into a flutter when the letter came. In another week Elizabeth's child would be with them.

"If only she isn't like her father," said Charlotte with foreboding, as she aired and swept the southeast spare room for their expected guest. They had three spare rooms at the Grange, but the aunts had selected the southeast one for their niece because it was done in white, "and white seems the most appropriate for a young girl," Ellen said, as she arranged a pitcher of wild roses on the table.

"I think everything is ready," announced Charlotte. "I put the very finest sheets on the bed, they smell deliciously of lavender, and we had very good luck doing up the muslin curtains. It is pleasant to be expecting a guest, isn't it, Ellen? I have often thought, although I have never said so before, that our lives were too self-centred. We seemed to have no interests outside of ourselves. Even Elizabeth has been really nothing to us, you know. She seemed to have become a stranger. I hope her child will be the means of bringing us nearer together again."

"If she has James Sheldon's round face and big blue eyes and curly yellow hair I shall never really like her, no matter how Ingelowish she may be inside," said Ellen decidedly.

When Worth Sheldon came, each of her aunts drew a long breath of relief. Worth was not in the least like her father in appearance. Neither did she resemble her mother, who had been a sprightly, black-haired and black-eyed girl. Worth was tall and straight, with a long braid of thick, wavy brown hair, large, level-gazing grey eyes, a square jaw, and an excellent chin with a dimple in it.

"She is the very image of Mother's sister, Aunt Alice, who died so long ago," said Charlotte. "You don't remember her, Ellen, but I do very well. She was the sweetest woman that ever drew breath. She was Paul's favourite aunt, too," Charlotte added with a sigh. Paul's antagonistic attitude was the only drawback to the joy of this meeting. How delightful it would have been if he had not refused to be there too, to welcome Elizabeth's child.

Worth came to hearts prepared to love her, but they must have loved her in any case. In a day Aunt Charlotte and Aunt Ellen and shy, quiet Uncle George had yielded wholly to her charm. She was girlishly bright and merry, frankly delighted with the old homestead and the quaint, old-fashioned, daintily kept rooms. Yet there was no suggestion of gush about her; she did not go into raptures, but her pleasure shone out in eyes and tones. There was so much to tell and ask and remember the first day that it was not until the second morning after her arrival that Worth asked the question her aunts had been dreading. She asked it out in the orchard, in the emerald gloom of a long arcade of stout old trees that Grandfather Ingelow had planted fifty years ago.

"Aunt Charlotte, when is Uncle Paul coming up to see me? I long to see him; Mother has talked so much to me about him. She was his favourite sister, wasn't she?"

Charlotte and Ellen looked at each other. Ellen nodded slyly. It would be better to tell Worth the whole truth at once. She would certainly find it out soon.

"I do not think, my dear," said Aunt Charlotte quietly, "that your Uncle Paul will be up to see you at all."

"Why not?" asked Worth, her serious grey eyes looking straight into Aunt Charlotte's troubled dark ones. Aunt Charlotte understood that Elizabeth had never told Worth anything about her family's resentment of her marriage. It was not a pleasant thing to have to explain it all to Elizabeth's child, but it must be done.

"I think, my dear," she said gently, "that I will have to tell you a little bit of our family history that may not be very pleasant to hear or tell. Perhaps you don't know that when your mother married we—we—did not exactly approve of her marriage. Perhaps we were mistaken; at any rate it was wrong and foolish to let it come between us and her as we have done. But that is how it was. None of us approved, as I have said, but none of us was so bitter as your Uncle Paul. Your mother was his favourite sister, and he was very deeply attached to her. She was only a year younger than he. When he bought the Greenwood farm she went and kept house for him for three years before her marriage. When she married, Paul was terribly angry. He was always a strange man, very determined and unyielding. He said he would never forgive her, and he never has. He has never married, and he has lived so long alone at Greenwood with only deaf old Mrs. Bree to keep house for him that he has grown odder than ever. One of us wanted to go and keep house for him, but he would not let us. And—I must tell you this although I hate to—he was very angry when he heard we had invited you to visit us, and he said he would not come near the Grange as long as you were here. Oh, you can't realize how bitter and obstinate he is. We pleaded with him, but I think that only made him worse. We have felt so bad over it, your Aunt Ellen and your Uncle George and I, but we can do nothing at all."

Worth had listened gravely. The story was all new to her, but she had long thought there must be a something at the root of her mother's indifferent relations with her old home and friends. When Aunt Charlotte, flushed and half-tearful, finished speaking, a little glimmer of fun came into Worth's grey eyes, and her dimple was very pronounced as she said,

"Then, if Uncle Paul will not come to see me, I must go to see him."

"My dear!" cried both her aunts together in dismay. Aunt Ellen got her breath first.

"Oh, my dear child, you must not think of such a thing," she cried nervously. "It would never do. He would—I don't know what he would do—order you off the premises, or say something dreadful. No! No! Wait. Perhaps he will come after all—we will see. You must have patience."

Worth shook her head and the smile in her eyes deepened.

"I don't think he will come," she said. "Mother has told me something about the Ingelow stubbornness. She says I have it in full measure, but I like to call it determination, it sounds so much better. No, the mountain will not come to Mohammed, so Mohammed will go to the mountain. I think I will walk down to Greenwood this afternoon. There, dear aunties, don't look so troubled. Uncle Paul won't run at me with a pitchfork, will he? He can't do worse than order me off his premises, as you say."

Aunt Charlotte shook her head. She understood that no argument would turn the girl from her purpose if she had the Ingelow will, so she said nothing more. In the afternoon Worth set out for Greenwood, a mile away.

"Oh, what will Paul say?" exclaimed the aunts, with dismal forebodings.

Worth met her Uncle Paul at the garden gate. He was standing there when she came up the slope of the long lane, a tall, massive figure of a man, with deep-set black eyes, a long, prematurely white beard, and a hooked nose. Handsome and stubborn enough Paul Ingelow looked. It was not without reason that his neighbours called him the oddest Ingelow of them all.

Behind him was a fine old farmhouse in beautiful grounds. Worth felt almost as much interested in Greenwood as in the Grange. It had been her mother's home for three years, and Elizabeth Ingelow had loved it and talked much to her daughter of it.

Paul Ingelow did not move or speak, although he probably guessed who his visitor was. Worth held out her hand. "How do you do, Uncle Paul?" she said.

Paul ignored the outstretched hand. "Who are you?" he asked gruffly.

"I am Worth Sheldon, your sister Elizabeth's daughter," she answered. "Won't you shake hands with me, Uncle Paul?"

"I have no sister Elizabeth," he answered unbendingly.

Worth folded her hands on the gatepost and met his frowning gaze unshrinkingly. "Oh, yes, you have," she said calmly. "You can't do away with natural ties by simply ignoring them, Uncle Paul. They go on existing. I never knew until this morning that you were at enmity with my mother. She never told me. But she has talked a great deal of you to me. She has told me often how much you and she loved each other and how good you always were to her. She sent her love to you."

"Years ago I had a sister Elizabeth," said Paul Ingelow harshly. "I loved her very tenderly, but she married against my will a shiftless scamp who—"

Worth lifted her hand slightly. "He was my father, Uncle Paul, and he was always kind to me; whatever his faults may have been I cannot listen to a word against him."

"You shouldn't have come here, then," he said, but he said it less harshly. There was even a certain reluctant approval of this composed, independent niece in his eyes. "Didn't they tell you at the Grange that I didn't want to see you?"

"Yes, they told me this morning, but *I* wanted to see you, so I came. Why cannot we be friends, Uncle Paul, not because we are uncle and niece, but simply because you are you and I am I? Let us leave my father and mother out of the question and start fair on our own account."

For a moment Uncle Paul looked at her. She met his gaze frankly and firmly, with a merry smile lurking in her eyes. Then he threw back his head and laughed a hearty laugh that was good to hear. "Very well," he said. "It is a bargain."

He put his hand over the gate and shook hers. Then he opened the gate and invited her into the house. Worth stayed to tea, and Uncle Paul showed her all over Greenwood.

"You are to come here as often as you like," he told her. "When a young lady and I make a compact of friendship I am going to live up to it. But you are not to talk to me about your mother. Remember, we are friends because I am I and you are you, and there is no question of anybody else."

The Grange Ingelows were amazed to see Paul bringing Worth home in his buggy that evening. When Worth had gone into the house Charlotte told him that she was glad to see that he had relented towards Elizabeth's child.

"I have not," he made stern answer. "I don't know whom you mean by Elizabeth's child. That young woman and I have taken a liking for each other which we mean to cultivate on our own account. Don't call her Elizabeth's child to me again."

As the days and weeks went by Worth grew dearer and dearer to the Grange folk. The aunts often wondered to themselves how they had existed before Worth came and, oftener yet, how they could do without her when the time came for her to go home. Meanwhile, the odd friendship between her and Uncle Paul deepened and grew. They read and drove and walked together. Worth spent half her time at Greenwood. Once Uncle Paul said to her, as if speaking half to himself,

"To think that James Sheldon could have a daughter like you!"

Up went Worth's head. Worth's grey eyes flashed. "I thought we were not to speak of my parents?" she said. "You ought not to have been the first to break the compact, Uncle Paul."

"I accept the rebuke and beg your pardon," he said. He liked her all the better for those little flashes of spirit across her girlish composure.

One day in September they were together in the garden at Greenwood. Worth, looking lovingly and regretfully down the sun-flecked avenue of box, said with a sigh, "Next month I must go home. How sorry I shall be to leave the Grange and Greenwood. I have had such a delightful summer, and I have learned to love all the old nooks and corners as well as if I had lived here all my life."

"Stay here!" said Uncle Paul abruptly. "Stay here with me. I want you, Worth. Let Greenwood be your home henceforth and adopt your crusty old bachelor uncle for a father."

"Oh, Uncle Paul," cried Worth, "I don't know—I don't think—oh, you surprise me!"

"I surprise myself, perhaps. But I mean it, Worth. I am a rich, lonely old man and I want to keep this new interest you have brought into my life. Stay with me. I will try to give you a very happy life, my child, and all I have shall be yours."

Seeing her troubled face, he added, "There, I don't ask you to decide right here. I suppose you have other claims to adjust. Take time to think it over."

"Thank you," said Worth. She went back to the Grange as one in a dream and shut herself up in the white southeast room to think. She knew that she wanted to accept this unexpected offer of Uncle Paul's. Worth's loyal tongue had never betrayed, even to the loving aunts, any discontent in the prairie farm life that had always been hers. But it had been a hard life for the girl, narrow and poverty-bounded. She longed to put forth her hand and take this other life which opened so temptingly before her. She knew, too, that her mother, ambitious for her child, would not be likely to interpose any objections. She had only to go to Uncle Paul and all that she longed for would be given her, together with the faithful, protecting fatherly love and care that in all its strength and sweetness had never been hers.

She must decide for herself. Not even of Aunt Charlotte or Aunt Ellen could she ask advice. She knew they would entreat her to accept, and she needed no such incentive to her own wishes. Far on into the night Worth sat at the white-curtained dormer window, looking at the stars over the apple trees, and fighting her battle between inclination and duty. It was a hard and stubbornly contested battle, but with that square chin and those unfaltering grey eyes it could end in only one way. Next day Worth went down to Greenwood.

"Well, what is it to be?" said Uncle Paul without preface, as he met her in the garden.

"I cannot come, Uncle Paul," said Worth steadily. "I cannot give up my mother."

"I don't ask you to give her up," he said gruffly. "You can write to her and visit her. I don't want to come between parent and child."

"That isn't the point exactly, Uncle Paul. I hope you will not be angry with me for not accepting your offer. I wanted to—you don't know how much I wanted to—but I cannot. Mother and I are so much to each other, Uncle Paul, more, I am sure, than even most mothers and daughters. You have never let me speak of her, but I must tell you this. Mother has often told me that when I came to her things were going very hard with her and that I was heaven's own gift to comfort and encourage her. Then, in the ten years that followed, the three other babies that came to her all died before they were two years old. And with each loss Mother said I grew dearer to her. Don't you see, Uncle Paul, I'm not merely just one child to her but I'm *all* those children? Six years ago the twins were born, and they are dear, bright little lads, but they are very small yet, so Mother has really nobody but me. I know she would consent to let me stay here, because she would think it best for me, but it wouldn't be really best for me; it couldn't be best for a girl to do what wasn't right. I love you, Uncle Paul, and I love Greenwood, and I want to stay so much, but I cannot. I have thought it all over and I must go back to Mother."

Uncle Paul did not say one word. He turned his back on Worth and walked the full length of the box alley twice. Worth watched him wistfully. Was he very angry? Would he forgive her?

"You are an Ingelow, Worth," he said when he came back. That was all, but Worth understood that her decision was not to cause any estrangement between them.

A month later Worth's last day at the Grange came. She was to leave for the West the next morning. They were all out in Grandfather Ingelow's arcade, Uncle George and Aunt Charlotte and Aunt Ellen and Worth, enjoying the ripe mellow sunshine of the October day, when Paul Ingelow came up the slope. Worth went to meet him with outstretched hands. He took them both in his and looked at her very gravely.

"I have not come to say goodbye, Worth. I will not say it. You are coming back to me."

Worth shook her brown head sadly. "Oh, I cannot, Uncle Paul. You know—I told you—"

"Yes, I know," he interrupted. "I have been thinking it all over every day since. You know yourself what the Ingelow determination is. It's a good thing in a good cause but a bad thing in a bad one. And it is no easy thing to conquer when you've let it rule you for years as I have done. But I have conquered it, or you have conquered it for me. Child, here is a letter. It is to your mother—my sister Elizabeth. In it I have asked her to forgive me, and to forget our long estrangement. I have asked her to come back to me with you and her boys. I want you all—all—at Greenwood and I will do the best I can for you all."

"Oh, Uncle Paul," cried Worth, her face aglow and quivering with smiles and tears and sunshine.

"Do you think she will forgive me and come?"

"I know she will," cried Worth. "I know how she has longed for you and home. Oh, I am so happy, Uncle Paul!"

He smiled at her and put his arm over her shoulder. Together they walked up the golden arcade to tell the others. That night Charlotte and Ellen cried with happiness as they talked it over in the twilight.

"How beautiful!" murmured Charlotte softly. "We shall not lose Worth after all. Ellen, I could not have borne it to see that girl go utterly out of our lives again."

"I always hoped and believed that Elizabeth's child would somehow bring us all together again," said Ellen happily.

Freda's Adopted Grave

North Point, where Freda lived, was the bleakest settlement in the world. Even its inhabitants, who loved it, had to admit that. The northeast winds swept whistling up the bay and blew rawly over the long hill that sloped down to it, blighting everything that was in their way. Only the sturdy firs and spruces could hold their own against it. So there were no orchards or groves or flower gardens in North Point.

Just over the hill, in a sheltered southwest valley, was the North Point church with the graveyard behind it, and this graveyard was the most beautiful spot in North Point or near it. The North Point folk loved flowers. They could not have them about their homes, so they had them in their graveyard. It was a matter of pride with each family to keep the separate plot neatly trimmed and weeded and adorned with beautiful blossoms.

It was one of the unwritten laws of the little community that on some selected day in May everybody would repair to the graveyard to plant, trim and clip. It was not an unpleasant duty, even to those whose sorrow was fresh. It seemed as if they were still doing something for the friends who had gone when they made their earthly resting places beautiful.

As for the children, they looked forward to "Graveyard Day" as a very delightful anniversary, and it divided its spring honours with the amount of the herring catch.

"Tomorrow is Graveyard Day," said Minnie Hutchinson at school recess, when all the little girls were sitting on the fence. "Ain't I glad! I've got the loveliest big white rosebush to plant by Grandma Hutchinson's grave. Uncle Robert sent it out from town."

"My mother has ten tuberoses to set out," said Nan Gray proudly.

"We're going to plant a row of lilies right around our plot," said Katie Morris.

Every little girl had some boast to make, that is, every little girl but Freda. Freda sat in a corner all by herself and felt miserably outside of everything. She had no part or lot in Graveyard Day.

"Are you going to plant anything, Freda?" asked Nan, with a wink at the others.

Freda shook her head mutely.

"Freda can't plant anything," said Winnie Bell cruelly, although she did not mean to be cruel. "She hasn't got a grave."

Just then Freda felt as if her gravelessness were a positive disgrace and crime, as if not to have an interest in a single grave in North Point cemetery branded you as an outcast forever and ever. It very nearly did in North Point. The other little girls pitied Freda, but at the same time they rather looked down upon her for it with the complacency of those who had been born into a good heritage of family graves and had an undisputed right to celebrate Graveyard Day.

Freda felt that her cup of wretchedness was full. She sat miserably on the fence while the other girls ran off to play, and she walked home alone at night. It seemed to her that she could *not* bear it any longer.

Freda was ten years old. Four years ago Mrs. Wilson had taken her from the orphan asylum in town. Mrs. Wilson lived just this side of the hill from the graveyard, and everybody in North Point called her a "crank." They pitied any child she took, they said. It would be worked to death and treated like a slave. At first they tried to pump Freda concerning Mrs. Wilson's treatment of her, but Freda was not to be pumped. She was a quiet little mite, with big, wistful dark eyes that had a disconcerting fashion of looking the gossips out of countenance. But if Freda had been disposed to complain, the North Point people would have found out that they had been only too correct in their predictions.

"Mrs. Wilson," Freda said timidly that night, "why haven't we got a grave?"

Mrs. Wilson averred that such a question gave her the "creeps."

"You ought to be very thankful that we haven't," she said severely. "That Graveyard Day is a heathenish custom, anyhow. They make a regular picnic of it, and it makes me sick to hear those school girls chattering about what they mean to plant, each one trying to outblow the other. If I *had* a grave there, I wouldn't make a flower garden of it!"

Freda did not go to the graveyard the next day, although it was a holiday. But in the evening, when everybody had gone home, she crept over the hill and through the beech grove to see what had been done.

The plots were all very neat and prettily set out with plants and bulbs. Some perennials were already in bud. The grave of Katie Morris' great-uncle, who had been dead for forty years, was covered with blossoming purple pansies. Every grave, no matter how small or old, had its share of promise—every grave except one. Freda came across it with a feeling of surprise. It was away down in the lower corner where there were no plots. It was shut off from the others by a growth of young poplars and was sunken and overgrown with blueberry shrubs. There was no headstone, and it looked dismally neglected. Freda felt a sympathy for it. She had no grave, and this grave had nobody to tend it or care for it.

When she went home she asked Mrs. Wilson whose it was.

"Humph!" said Mrs. Wilson. "If you have so much spare time lying round loose, you'd better put it into your sewing instead of prowling about graveyards. Do you expect me to work my fingers to the bone making clothes for you? I wish I'd left you in the asylum. That grave is Jordan Slade's, I suppose. He died twenty years ago, and a worthless, drunken scamp he was. He served a term in the penitentiary for breaking into Andrew Messervey's store, and after it he had the face to come back to North Point. But respectable people would have nothing to do with him, and he went to the dogs altogether—had to be buried on charity when he died. He hasn't any relations here. There was a sister, a little girl of ten, who used to live with the Cogswells over at East Point. After Jord died, some rich folks saw her and was so struck with her good looks that they took her away with them. I don't know what become of her, and I don't care. Go and bring the cows up."

When Freda went to bed that night her mind was made up. She would adopt Jordan Slade's grave.

Thereafter, Freda spent her few precious spare-time moments in the graveyard. She clipped the blueberry shrubs and long, tangled grasses from the grave with a pair of rusty old shears that blistered her little brown hands badly. She brought ferns from the woods to plant about it. She begged a root of heliotrope from Nan Gray, a clump of day lilies from Katie Morris, a rosebush slip from Nellie Bell, some pansy seed from old Mrs. Bennett, and a geranium shoot from Minnie Hutchinson's big sister. She planted, weeded and watered faithfully, and her efforts were rewarded. "Her" grave soon looked as nice as any in the graveyard.

Nobody but Freda knew about it. The poplar growth concealed the corner from sight, and everybody had quite forgotten poor, disreputable Jordan Slade's grave. At least, it seemed as if everybody had. But one evening, when Freda slipped down to the graveyard with a little can of water and rounded the corner of the poplars, she saw a lady standing by the grave—a strange lady dressed in black, with the loveliest face Freda had ever seen, and tears in her eyes.

The lady gave a little start when she saw Freda with her can of water.

"Can you tell me who has been looking after this grave?" she said.

"It—it was I," faltered Freda, wondering if the lady would be angry with her. "Pleas'm, it was I, but I didn't mean any harm. All the other little girls had a grave, and I hadn't any, so I just adopted this one."

"Did you know whose it was?" asked the lady gently.

"Yes'm—Jordan Slade's. Mrs. Wilson told me."

"Jordan Slade was my brother," said the lady. "He went sadly astray, but he was not all bad. He was weak and too easily influenced. But whatever his faults, he was good and kind—oh! so good and kind—to me when I was a child. I loved him with all my heart. It has always been my wish to come back and visit his grave, but I have never been able to come, my home has been so far away. I expected to find it neglected. I cannot tell you how pleased and touched I am to find it kept so beautifully. Thank you over and over again, my dear child!"

"Then you're not cross, ma'am?" said Freda eagerly. "And I may go on looking after it, may I? Oh, it just seems as if I couldn't bear not to!"

"You may look after it as long as you want to, my dear. I will help you, too. I am to be at East Point all summer. This will be our grave—yours and mine."

That summer was a wonderful one for Freda. She had found a firm friend in Mrs. Halliday. The latter was a wealthy woman. Her husband had died a short time previously and she had no children. When she went away in the fall, Freda went with her "to be her own little girl for always." Mrs. Wilson consented grudgingly to give Freda up, although she grumbled a great deal about ingratitude.

Before they went they paid a farewell visit to their grave. Mrs. Halliday had arranged with some of the North Point people to keep it well attended to, but Freda cried at leaving it.

"Don't feel badly about it, dear," comforted Mrs. Halliday. "We are coming back every summer to see it. It will always be our grave."

Freda slipped her hand into Mrs. Halliday's and smiled up at her.

"I'd never have found you, Aunty, if it hadn't been for this grave," she said happily. "I'm so glad I adopted it."

How Don Was Saved

Will Barrie went whistling down the lane of the Locksley farm, took a short cut over a field of clover aftermath and through a sloping orchard where the trees were laden with apples, and emerged into the farmhouse yard where Curtis Locksley was sitting on a pile of logs, idly whittling at a stick.

"You look as if you had a corner in time, Curt," said Will. "I call that luck, for I want you to go chestnutting up to Grier's Hill with me. I met old Tom Grier on the road yesterday, and he told me I might go any day. Nice old man, Tom Grier."

"Good!" said Curtis heartily, as he sprang up. "If I haven't exactly a corner in time, I have a day off, at least. Uncle doesn't need me today. Wait till I whistle for Don. May as well take him with us."

Curtis whistled accordingly, but Don, his handsome Newfoundland dog, did not appear. After calling and whistling about the yard and barns for several minutes, Curtis turned away disappointedly.

"He can't be anywhere around. It is very strange. Don never used to go away from home without me, but lately he has been missing several times, and twice last week he wasn't here in the morning and didn't turn up until midday."

"I'd keep him shut up until I broke him of the habit of playing truant, if I were you," said Will, as they turned into the lane.

"Don hates to be shut up, howls all the time so mournfully that I can't stand it," responded Curtis.

"Well," said Will, hesitatingly, "maybe that would be better after all than letting him stray away with other dogs who may teach him bad habits. I saw Don myself one evening last week ambling down the Harbour road with that big brown dog of Sam Ventnor's. Ventnor's dog is beginning to have a bad reputation, you know. There have been several sheep worried lately, and—"

"Don wouldn't touch a sheep!" interrupted Curtis hotly.

"I daresay not, not yet. But Ventnor's dog is under suspicion, and if Don runs with him he'll learn the trick sure as preaching. The farmers are growling a good bit already, and if they hear of Don and Ventnor's dog going about in company, they'll put it on them both. Better keep Don shut up awhile, let him howl as he likes."

"I believe I will," said Curtis soberly. "I don't want Don to fall under suspicion of sheep-worrying, though I'm sure he would never do it. Anyhow, I don't want him to run with Ventnor's dog. I'll chain him up in the barn when I go home. I couldn't stand it if anything happened to Don. After you, he's the only chum I've got—and he's a good one."

Will agreed. He was almost as fond of Don as Curtis was. But he did not feel so sure that the dog would not worry a sheep. Will knew that Don was suspected already, but he did not like to tell Curtis so. And of course there was as yet no positive proof—merely mutterings and suggestions among the Bayside farmers who had lost sheep and were anxious to locate their slayer. There were many other dogs in Bayside and the surrounding districts who were just as likely to be the guilty animals, and Will hoped that if Don were shut up for a time, suspicion might be averted from him, especially if the worryings still went on.

He had felt a little doubtful about hinting the truth to Curtis, who was a high-spirited lad and always resented any slur cast upon Don much more bitterly than if it were meant for himself. But he knew that Curtis would take it better from him than from the other Bayside boys, one or the other of whom would be sure soon to cast something up to Curtis about his dog. Will felt decidedly relieved to find that Curtis took his advice in the spirit in which it was offered.

"Who have lost sheep lately?" queried Curtis, as they left the main road and struck into a wood path through the ranks of beeches on Tom Grier's land.

"Nearly everybody on the Hollow farms," answered Will. "Until last week nobody on the Hill farms had lost any. But Tuesday night old Paul Stockton had six fine sheep killed in his upland pasture behind the fir woods. He is furious about it, I believe, and vows he'll find out what dog did it and have him shot."

Curtis looked grave. Paul Stockton's farm was only about a quarter of a mile from the Locksley homestead, and he knew that Paul had an old family grudge against his Uncle Arnold, which included his nephew and all belonging to him. Moreover, Curtis remembered with a sinking heart that Wednesday morning had been one of the mornings upon which Don was missing.

"But I don't care!" he thought miserably. "I know Don didn't kill those sheep."

"Talking of old Paul," said Will, who thought it advisable to turn the conversation, "reminds me that they are getting anxious at the Harbour about George Finley's schooner, the *Amy Reade*. She was due three days ago and there's no sign of her yet. And there have been two bad gales since she left Morro. Oscar Stockton is on board of her, you know, and his father is worried about him. There are five other men on her, all from the Harbour, and their folks down there are pretty wild about the schooner."

Nothing more was said about the sheep, and soon, in the pleasures of chestnutting, Curtis forgot his anxiety. Old Tom Grier had called to the boys as they passed his house to come back and have dinner there when the time came. This they did, and it was late in the afternoon when Curtis, with his bag of chestnuts over his shoulder, walked into the Locksley yard.

His uncle was standing before the open barn doors, talking to an elderly, grizzled man with a thin, shrewd face.

Curtis's heart sank as he recognized old Paul Stockton. What could have brought him over?

"Curtis," called his uncle, "come here."

As Curtis crossed the yard, Don came bounding down the slope from the house to meet him. He put his hand on the dog's big head and the two of them walked slowly to the barn. Old Paul included them both in a vindictive scowl.

"Curtis," said his uncle gravely, "here's a bad business. Mr. Stockton tells me that your dog has been worrying his sheep."

"It's a—" began Curtis angrily. Then he checked himself and went on more calmly.

"That can't be so, Mr. Stockton. My dog would not harm anything."

"He killed or helped to kill six of the finest sheep in my flock!" retorted old Paul.

"What proof have you of it?" demanded Curtis, trying to keep his anger within bounds.

"Abner Peck saw your dog and Ventnor's running together through my sheep pasture at sundown on Tuesday evening," answered old Paul. "Wednesday morning I found this in the corner of the pasture where the sheep were worried. Your uncle admits that it was tied around your dog's neck on Tuesday."

And old Paul held out triumphantly a faded red ribbon. Curtis recognized it at a glance. It was the ribbon his little cousin, Lena, had tied around Don's neck Tuesday afternoon. He remembered how they had laughed at the effect of that frivolous red collar and bow on Don's massive body.

"I'm sure Don isn't guilty!" he cried passionately.

Mr. Locksley shook his head.

"I'm afraid he is, Curtis. The case looks very black against him, and sheep-stealing is a serious offence."

"The dog must be shot," said old Paul decidedly. "I leave the matter in your hands, Mr. Locksley. I've got enough proof to convict the dog and, if you don't have him killed, I'll make you pay for the sheep he worried."

As old Paul strode away, Curtis looked beseechingly at his uncle.

"Don mustn't be shot, Uncle!" he said desperately. "I'll chain him up all the time."

"And have him howling night and day as if we had a brood of banshees about the place?" said Mr. Locksley sarcastically. He was a stern man with little sentiment in his nature and no understanding whatever of Curtis's affection for Don. The Bayside people said that Arnold Locksley had always been very severe with his nephew. "No, no, Curtis, you must look at the matter sensibly. The dog is a nuisance and must be shot. You can't keep him shut up forever, and, if he has once learned the trick of sheep-worrying, he will never forget it. You can get another dog if you must have one. I'll get Charles Pippey to come and shoot Don tomorrow. No sulking now, Curtis. You are too big a boy for that. Tie the dog up for the night and then go and put the calves in. There is a storm coming. The wind is blowing hard from the northeast now."

His uncle walked away, leaving the boy white and miserable in the yard. He looked at Don, who sat on his haunches and returned his gaze frankly and open-heartedly. He did not look like a guilty dog. Could it be possible that he had really worried those sheep?

"I'll never believe it of you, old fellow!" Curtis said, as he led the dog into a corner of the carriage house and tied him up there. Then he flung himself down on a pile of sacks beside him and buried his face in Don's curly black fur. The boy felt sullen, rebellious and wretched.

He lay there until dark, thinking his own bitter thoughts and listening to the rapidly increasing gale. Finally he got up and flung off after the calves, with Don's melancholy howls at finding himself deserted ringing in his ears.

He'll be quiet enough tomorrow night, thought Curtis wretchedly, as he went upstairs to bed after housing the calves. For a long while he lay awake, but finally dropped into a heavy slumber which lasted until his aunt called him for milking.

The wind was blowing more furiously than ever. Up over the fields came the roar and crash of the surges on the outside shore. The Harbour to the east of Bayside was rough and stormy.

They were just rising from breakfast when Will Barrie burst into the kitchen.

"The *Amy Reade* is ashore on Gleeson's rocks!" he shouted. "Struck there at daylight this morning! Come on, Curt!"

Curtis sprang for his cap, his uncle following suit more deliberately. As the two boys ran through the yard, Curtis heard Don howling.

"I'll take him with me!" he muttered. "Wait a minute, Will."

The Harbour road was thronged with people hurrying to the outside shore, for the news of the *Amy Readers* disaster had spread rapidly. As the boys, with the rejoicing Don at their heels, pelted along, Sam Morrow overtook them in a cart and told them to jump in. Sam had already been down to the shore and had gone back to tell his father. As they jolted along, he screamed information at them over the shriek of the gale.

"Bad business, this! She's pounding on a reef 'bout a quarter of a mile out. They're sure she's going to break up—old tub, you know—leaky—rotten. The sea's tremenjus high, and the surfs going dean over her. There can't be no boat launched for hours yet—they'll all be drowned. Old Paul's down there like a madman—offering everything he's got to the man who'll save Oscar, but it can't be done."

By this time they had reached the shore, which was black with excited people. Out on Gleeson's Reef the ill-fated little schooner was visible amid the flying spray. A grizzled old Harbour fisherman, to whom Sam shouted a question, shook his head.

"No, can't do nothin'! No boat c'd live in that surf f'r a moment. The schooner'll go to pieces mighty soon, I'm feared. It's turrible! turrible! to stan' by an' watch yer neighbours drown like this!"

Curtis and Will elbowed their way down to the water's edge. The relatives of the crew were all there in various stages of despair, but old Paul Stockton seemed like a man demented. He ran up and down the beach, crying and praying. His only son was on the *Amy Reade*, and he could do nothing to save him!

"What are they doing?" asked Will of Martin Clark.

"Trying to get a line ashore by throwing out a small rope with a stick tied to it," answered Martin. "It's young Stockton that's trying now. But it isn't any use. The cross-currents on that reef are too powerful."

"Why, Don will bring that line ashore!" exclaimed Curtis. "Here, Don! Don, I say!"

The dog bounded back along the shore with a quick bark. Curtis grasped him by the collar and pointed to the stick which young Stockton had just hurled again into the water. Don, with another bark of comprehension, dashed into the sea. The onlookers, grasping the situation, gave a cheer and then relapsed into silence. Only the shriek of the gale and the crash of the waves could be heard as they watched the magnificent dog swimming out through the breakers, his big black head now rising on the crest of a wave and now disappearing in the hollow behind it. When Don finally reached the tossing stick, grasped it in his mouth and turned shoreward, another great shout went up from the beach. A woman behind Curtis, whose husband was on the schooner, dropped on her knees on the pebbles, sobbing and thanking God. Curtis himself felt the stinging tears start to his eyes.

When Don reached the shore he dropped the stick at Curtis's feet and gave himself a tremendous shake. Curtis caught at the stick, while a dozen men and women threw themselves bodily on Don, hugging him and kissing his wet fur like distracted creatures. Old Paul Stockton was among them. Over his shoulder Don's big black head looked up, his eyes asking as plainly as speech what all this fuss was about.

Meanwhile some of the men had already pulled a big hawser ashore and made it fast. In half an hour the crew of the *Amy Reade* were safe on shore, chilled and dripping. Before they were hurried away to warmth and shelter, old Paul Stockton caught Curtis's hand. The tears were running freely down his hard, old face.

"Tell your uncle he is not to lay a finger on that dog!" he said. "He never killed a sheep of mine—he couldn't! And if he did I don't care! He's welcome to kill them all, if nothing but mutton'll serve his turn."

Curtis walked home with a glad heart. Mr. Locksley heard old Paul's message with a smile. He, too, had been touched by Don's splendid feat.

"Well, Curtis, I'm very glad that it has turned old Paul in his favour. But we must shut Don up for a week or so, no matter how hard he takes it. You can see that for yourself. After all, he might have worried the sheep. And, anyway, he must be broken of his intimacy with Ventnor's dog."

Curtis acknowledged the justice of this and poor Don was tied up again. His captivity was not long, however, for Ventnor's dog was soon shot. When Don was released, Curtis had an anxious time for a week or two. But no more sheep were worried, and Don's innocence was triumphantly established. As for old Paul Stockton, it seemed as if he could not do enough for Curtis and Don. His ancient grudge against the Locksleys was completely forgotten, and from that date he was a firm friend of Curtis. In regard to Don, old Paul would say:

"Why, there never was such a dog before, sir, never! He just talks with his eyes, that dog does. And if you'd just 'a' seen him swimming out to that schooner! Bones? Yes, sir! Every time that dog comes here he's to get the best bones we've got for him—and more'n bones, too. That dog's a hero, sir, that's what he is!"

Miss Madeline's Proposal

"Auntie, I have something to tell you," said Lina, with a blush that made her look more than ever like one of the climbing roses that nodded about the windows of the "old Churchill place," as it was always called in Lower Wentworth.

Miss Madeline, sitting in the low rocker by the parlour window, seemed like the presiding genius of the place. Everything about her matched her sweet old-fashionedness, from the crown of her soft brown hair, dressed in the style of her long ago girlhood, to the toes of her daintily slippered feet. Outside of the old Churchill place, in the busy streets of the up-to-date little town, Miss Madeline might have seemed out of harmony with her surroundings. But here, in this dim room, faintly scented with whiffs from the rose garden outside, she was like a note in some sweet, perfect melody of old time.

Lina, sitting on a little stool at Miss Madeline's feet with her curly head in her aunt's lap, was as pretty as Miss Madeline herself had once been. She was also very happy, and her happiness seemed to envelop her as in an atmosphere and lend her a new radiance and charm. Miss Madeline loved her pretty niece very dearly and patted the curly head tenderly with her slender white hands.

"What is it, my dear?"

"I'm—I'm engaged," whispered Lina, hiding her face in Miss Madeline's flowered muslin lap.

"Engaged!" Miss Madeline's tone was one of surprise and awe. She blushed as she said the word as deeply as Lina had done. Then she went on, with a little quiver of excitement in her voice, "To whom, my dear?"

"Oh, you don't know him, Auntie, but I hope you will soon. His name is Ralph Wylde. Isn't it pretty? I met him last winter, and we became very good friends. But we had a quarrel before I came down here and, oh, I have been so unhappy over it. Three weeks ago he wrote me and begged my pardon—so nice of him, because I was really all to blame, you know. And he said he loved me and—all that, you know."

"No, I don't know," said Miss Madeline gently. "But—but—I can imagine."

"Oh, I was so happy. I wrote back and I had this letter from him today. He is coming down tomorrow. You'll be glad to see him, won't you, Auntie?"

"Oh, yes, my dear, and I am glad for your sake—very glad. You are sure you love him?"

"Yes, indeed," said Lina, with a little laugh, as if wondering how anyone could doubt it.

Presently, Miss Madeline said in a shy voice, "Lina, did—did you ever receive a proposal of marriage from anybody besides Mr. Wylde?"

Lina laughed roguishly. "Why, yes, Auntie, ever so many. A dozen, at least."

"Oh, my dear!" cried Miss Madeline in a slightly shocked tone.

"But I did, really. Sometimes it was horrid and sometimes it was funny. It all depended on the man. Dear me, how red and uncomfortable most of them looked—all but the fifth. He was so cool and business like that he almost surprised me into accepting him."

"And—and what did you feel like, Lina?"

"Oh, frightened, mostly—but I always wanted to laugh too. You must know how it is yourself, Auntie. What did you feel like when somebody proposed to you?"

Miss Madeline flushed from chin to brow.

"Oh, Lina," she faltered as if she were confessing something very disgraceful, yet to which she was impelled by her strict truthfulness, "I—I—never had a proposal in my life—not one."

Lina opened her big brown eyes in amazement. "Why, Aunt Madeline! And you so pretty! What was the reason?"

"I've often wondered," said Miss Madeline faintly. "I *was* pretty, as you say—it's so long ago I can say that now. And I had many gentlemen friends. But nobody ever wanted to marry me. I sometimes wish that—that I could have had just one proposal. Not that I wanted to marry, you know, I do not mean that, but just so that it wouldn't have seemed that I was different from anybody else. It is very foolish of me to wish it, I know, and even wicked—for if I had not cared for the person it would have made him very unhappy. But then, he would have forgotten and I would have remembered. It would always have been something to be a little proud of."

"Yes," said Lina absently; her thoughts had gone back to Ralph.

That evening a letter was left at the front door of the old Churchill place. It was addressed in a scholarly hand to Miss Madeline Churchill, and Amelia Kent took it in. Amelia had been Miss Madeline's "help" for years and had grown grey in her service. In Amelia's loyal eyes Miss Madeline was still young and beautiful; she never doubted that the letter was for her mistress. Nobody else there was ever addressed as "Miss Madeline."

Miss Madeline was sitting by the window of her own room watching the sunset through the elms and reading her evening portion of Thomas à Kempis. She never liked to be disturbed when so employed but she read her letter after Amelia had gone out.

When she came to a certain paragraph, she turned very pale and Thomas à Kempis fell to the floor unheeded. When she had finished the letter she laid it on her lap, clasped her hands, and said, "Oh, oh, oh," in a faint, tremulous voice. Her cheeks were very pink and her eyes very bright. She did not even pick up Thomas à Kempis but went to the door and called Lina.

"What is it, Auntie?" asked Lina curiously, noticing the signs of unusual excitement about Miss Madeline.

Miss Madeline held out her letter with a trembling hand.

"Lina, dear, this is a letter from the Rev. Cecil Thorne. It—it is—a proposal of marriage. I feel terribly upset. How very strange that it should come so soon after our talk this morning! I want you to read it! Perhaps I ought not to show it to anyone—but I would like you to see it."

Lina took the letter and read it through. It was unmistakably a proposal of marriage and was, moreover, a very charming epistle of its kind, albeit a little stiff and old-fashioned.

"How funny!" said Lina when she came to the end.

"Funny!" exclaimed Miss Madeline, with a trace of indignation in her gentle voice.

"Oh, I didn't mean that the letter was funny," Lina hastened to explain, "only that, as you said, it is odd to think of it coming so soon after our talk."

But this was a little fib on Lina's part. She *had* thought that the letter or, rather, the fact that it had been written to Miss Madeline, funny. The Rev. Cecil Thorne was Miss Madeline's pastor. He was a handsome, scholarly man of middle age, and Lina had seen a good deal of him during her summer in Lower Wentworth. She had taught the infant class in Sunday School and sometimes she had thought that the minister was in love with her. But she must have been mistaken, she reflected; it must have been her aunt after all, and the Rev. Cecil Thorne's shyly displayed interest in her must have been purely professional.

"What a goose I was to be afraid he was in love with me!" she thought. Aloud she said, "He says he will call tomorrow evening to receive your answer."

"And, oh, what can I say to him?" murmured Miss Madeline in dismay. She wished she had a little of Lina's experience.

"You are going to—you will accept him, won't you?" asked Lina curiously.

"Oh, my dear, no!" cried Miss Madeline almost vehemently. "I couldn't think of such a thing. I am very sorry; do you think he will feel badly?"

"Judging from his letter I feel sure he will," said Lina decidedly.

Miss Madeline sighed. "Oh, dear me! It is very unpleasant. But of course I must refuse him. What a beautiful letter he writes too. I feel very much disturbed by this."

Miss Madeline picked up Thomas à Kempis, smoothed him out repentantly, and placed the letter between his leaves.

When the Rev. Cecil Thorne called at the old Churchill place next evening at sunset and asked for Miss Madeline Churchill, Amelia showed him into the parlour and went to call her mistress. Mr. Thorne sat down by the window that looked out on the lawn. His heart gave a bound as he caught a glimpse of an airy white muslin among the trees and a ripple of distant laughter. The next minute Lina appeared, strolling down the secluded path that curved about the birches. A young man was walking beside her with his arm around her. They crossed the green square before the house and disappeared in the rose garden.

Mr. Thorne leaned back in his chair and put his hand over his eyes. He felt that he had received his answer, and it was a very bitter moment for him. He had hardly dared hope that this bright, beautiful child could care for him, yet the realization came home to him none the less keenly. When Miss Madeline, paling and flushing by turns, came shyly in he had recovered his self-control sufficiently to be able to say "good evening" in a calm voice.

Miss Madeline sat down opposite to him. At that moment she was devoutly thankful that she had never had any other proposal to refuse.

It was a dreadful ordeal. If he would only help her out! But he did not speak and every moment of silence made it worse.

"I—received your letter, Mr. Thorne," she faltered at last, looking distressfully down at the floor.

"My letter!" Mr. Thorne turned towards her. In her agitation Miss Madeline did not notice the surprise in his face and tone.

"Yes," she said, gaining a little courage since the ice was broken. "It—it—was a very great surprise to me. I never thought you—you cared for me as—as you said. And I am very sorry because—because I cannot return your affection. And so, of course, I cannot marry you."

Mr. Thorne put his hand over his eyes again. He understood now that there had been some mistake and that Miss Madeline had received the letter he had written to her niece. Well, it did not matter—the appearance of the young man in the garden had settled that. Would he tell Miss Madeline of her mistake? No, it would only humiliate her and it made no difference, since she had refused him.

"I suppose it is of no use to ask you to reconsider your decision?" he said.

"Oh, no," cried Miss Madeline almost aghast. She was afraid he might ask it after all. "Not in the least use. I am sorry—so very sorry—but I could not answer differently. We—I hope—this will make no difference in our friendly relations, Mr. Thorne?"

"Not at all," said Mr. Thorne gravely. "We will try to forget that it has happened."

He bowed sadly and went out. Miss Madeline watched him guiltily as he walked across the lawn. He looked heart-broken. How dreadful it had been! And Lina had refused twelve men! How could she have lived through it?

"Perhaps one gets accustomed to doing it," reflected Miss Madeline. "But I am sure I never could."

"Did Mr. Thorne feel very badly?" whispered Lina that night.

"I'm afraid he did," confessed Miss Madeline sorrowfully. "He looked so pale and sad, Lina, that my heart ached for him. I am very thankful that I have never had any other proposals to decline. It is a very unpleasant experience. But," she added, with a little tinge of satisfaction in her sweet voice, "I am glad I had one. It—it has made me feel more like other people, you know, dear."

Miss Sally's Company

"How beautiful!" said Mary Seymour delightedly, as they dismounted from their wheels on the crest of the hill. "Ida, who could have supposed that such a view would be our reward for climbing that long, tedious hill with its ruts and stones? Don't you feel repaid?"

"Yes, but I am dreadfully thirsty," said Ida, who was always practical and never as enthusiastic over anything as Mary was. Yet she, too, felt a keen pleasure in the beauty of the scene before them. Almost at their feet lay the sea, creaming and shimmering in the mellow sunshine. Beyond, on either hand, stretched rugged brown cliffs and rocks, here running out to sea in misty purple headlands, there curving into bays and coves that seemed filled up with sunlight and glamour and pearly hazes; a beautiful shore and, seemingly, a lonely one. The only house visible from where the girls stood was a tiny grey one, with odd, low eaves and big chimneys, that stood down in the little valley on their right, where the cliffs broke away to let a brook run out to sea and formed a small cove, on whose sandy shore the waves lapped and crooned within a stone's throw of the house. On either side of the cove a headland made out to sea, curving around to enclose the sparkling water as in a cup.

"What a picturesque spot!" said Mary.

"But what a lonely one!" protested Ida. "Why, there isn't another house in sight. I wonder who lives in it. Anyway, I'm going down to ask them for a drink of water."

"I'd like to ask for a square meal, too," said Mary, laughing. "I am discovering that I am hungry. Fine scenery is very satisfying to the soul, to be sure, but it doesn't still the cravings of the inner girl. And we've wheeled ten miles this afternoon. I'm getting hungrier every minute."

They reached the little grey house by way of a sloping, grassy lane. Everything about it was very neat and trim. In front a white-washed paling shut in the garden which, sheltered as it was by the house, was ablaze with poppies and hollyhocks and geraniums. A path, bordered by big white clam shells, led through it to the front door, whose steps were slabs of smooth red sandstone from the beach.

"No children here, certainly," whispered Ida. "Every one of those clam shells is placed just so. And this walk is swept every day. No, we shall never dare to ask for anything to eat here. They would be afraid of our scattering crumbs."

Ida lifted her hand to knock, but before she could do so, the door was thrown open and a breathless little lady appeared on the threshold.

She was very small, with an eager, delicately featured face and dark eyes twinkling behind gold-rimmed glasses. She was dressed immaculately in an old-fashioned gown of grey silk with a white muslin fichu crossed over her shoulders, and her silvery hair fell on each side of her face in long, smooth curls that just touched her shoulders and bobbed and fluttered with her every motion; behind, it was caught up in a knot on her head and surmounted by a tiny lace cap.

She looks as if she had just stepped out of a bandbox of last century, thought Mary.

"Are you Cousin Abner's girls?" demanded the little lady eagerly. There was such excitement and expectation in her face and voice that both the Seymour girls felt uncomfortably that they ought to be "Cousin Abner's girls."

"No," said Mary reluctantly, "we're not. We are only—Martin Seymour's girls."

All the light went out of the little lady's face, as if some illuminating lamp had suddenly been quenched behind it. She seemed fairly to droop under her disappointment. As for the rest, the name of Martin Seymour evidently conveyed no especial meaning to her ears. How could she know that he was a multi-millionaire who was popularly supposed to breakfast on railroads and lunch on small corporations, and that his daughters were girls whom all people delighted to honour?

"No, of course you are not Cousin Abner's girls," she said sorrowfully. "I'd have known you couldn't be if I had just stopped to think. Because you are dark and they would be fair, of course; Cousin Abner and his wife were both fair. But when I saw you coming down the lane—I was peeking through the hall window upstairs, you know, I and Juliana—I was sure you were Helen and Beatrice at last. And I can't help wishing you were!"

"I wish we were, too, since you expected them," said Mary, smiling. "But—"

"Oh, I wasn't really expecting them," broke in the little lady. "Only I am always hoping that they will come. They never have yet, but Trenton isn't so very far away, and it is so lonely here. I just long for company—I and Juliana—and I thought I was going to have it today. Cousin Abner came to see me once since I moved here and he said the girls would come, too, but that was six months ago and they haven't come yet. But perhaps they will soon. It is always something to look forward to, you know."

She talked in a sweet, chirpy voice like a bird's. There were pathetic notes in it, too, as the girls instinctively felt. How very quaint and sweet and unworldly she was! Mary found herself feeling indignant at Cousin Abner's girls, whoever they were, for their neglect.

"We are out for a spin on our wheels," said Ida, "and we are very thirsty. We thought perhaps you would be kind enough to give us a drink of water."

"Oh, my dear, anything—anything I have is at your service," said the little lady delightedly. "If you will come in, I will get you some lemonade."

"I am afraid it is too much trouble," began Mary.

"Oh, no, no," cried the little lady. "It is a pleasure. I love doing things for people, I wish more of them would come to give me the chance. I never have any company, and I do so long for it. It's very lonesome here at Golden Gate. Oh, if you would only stay to tea with me, it would make me so happy. I am all prepared. I prepare every Saturday morning, in particular, so that if Cousin Abner's girls did come, I would be all ready. And when nobody comes, Juliana and I have to eat everything up ourselves. And that is bad for us—it gives Juliana indigestion. If you would only stay!"

"We will," agreed Ida promptly. "And we're glad of the chance. We are both terribly hungry, and it is very good of you to ask us."

"Oh, indeed, it isn't! It's just selfishness in me, that's what it is, pure selfishness! I want company so much. Come in, my dears, and I suppose I must introduce myself because you don't know me, do you now? I'm Miss Sally Temple, and this is Golden Gate Cottage. Dear me, this *is* something like living. You are special providences, that you are, indeed!"

She whisked them through a quaint little parlour, where everything was as dainty and neat and old-fashioned as herself, and into a spare bedroom beyond it, to put off their hats.

"Now, just excuse me a minute while I run out and tell Juliana that we are going to have company to tea. She will be so glad, Juliana will. Make yourselves at home, my dears."

"Isn't she delicious?" said Mary, when Miss Sally had tripped out. "I'd like to shake Cousin Abner's girls. This is what Dot Halliday would call an adventure, Ida."

"Isn't it! Miss Sally and this quaint old spot both seem like a chapter out of the novels our grandmothers cried over. Look here, Mary, she is lonely and our visit seems like a treat to her. Let us try to make it one. Let's just chum with her and tell her all about ourselves and our amusements and our dresses. That sounds frivolous, but you know what I mean. She'll like it. Let's be company in real earnest for her."

When Miss Sally came back, she was attended by Juliana carrying a tray of lemonade glasses. Juliana proved to be a diminutive lass of about fourteen whose cheerful, freckled face wore an expansive grin of pleasure. Evidently Juliana was as fond of "company" as her mistress was. Afterwards, the girls overheard a subdued colloquy between Miss Sally and Juliana out in the hall.

"Go set the table, Juliana, and put on Grandmother Temple's wedding china—be sure you dust it carefully—and the best tablecloth—and be sure you get the crease straight—and put some sweet peas in the centre—and be sure they are fresh. I want everything extra nice, Juliana."

"Yes'm, Miss Sally, I'll see to it. Isn't it great to have company, Miss Sally?" whispered Juliana.

The Seymour girls long remembered that tea table and the delicacies with which it was heaped. Privately, they did not wonder that Juliana had indigestion when she had to eat many such unaided. Being hungry, they did full justice to Miss Sally's good things, much to that little lady's delight.

She told them all about herself. She had lived at Golden Gate Cottage only a year.

"Before that, I lived away down the country at Millbridge with a cousin. My Uncle Ephraim owned Golden Gate Cottage, and when he died he left it to me and I came here to live. It is a pretty place, isn't it? You see those two headlands out there? In the morning, when the sun rises, the water between them is just a sea of gold, and that is why Uncle Ephraim had a fancy to call his place Golden Gate. I love it here. It is so nice to have a home of my own. I would be quite content if I had more company. But I have you today, and perhaps Beatrice and Helen will come next week. So I've really a great deal to be thankful for."

"What is your Cousin Abner's other name?" asked Mary, with a vague recollection of hearing of Beatrice and Helen—somebody—in Trenton.

"Reed—Abner Abimelech Reed," answered Miss Sally promptly. "A.A. Reed, he signs himself now. He is very well-to-do, I am told, and he carries on business in town. He was a very fine young man, my Cousin Abner. I don't know his wife."

Mary and Ida exchanged glances. Beatrice and Helen Reed! They knew them slightly as the daughters of a new-rich family who were hangers-on of the fashionable society in Trenton. They were regarded as decidedly vulgar, and so far their efforts to gain an entry into the exclusive circle where the Seymours and their like revolved had not been very successful.

"I'm afraid Miss Sally will wait a long while before she sees Cousin Abner's girls," said Mary, when they had gone back to the parlour and Miss Sally had excused herself to superintend the washing of Grandmother Temple's wedding china. "They probably look on her as a poor relation to be ignored altogether; whereas, if they were only like her, Trenton society would have made a place for them long ago."

The Seymour girls enjoyed that visit as much as Miss Sally did. She was eager to hear all about their girlish lives and amusements. They told her of their travels, of famous men and women they had seen, of parties they had attended, the dresses they wore, the little fads and hobbies of their set—all jumbled up together and all listened to eagerly by Miss Sally and also by Juliana, who was permitted to sit on the stairs out in the hall and so gather in the crumbs of this intellectual feast.

"Oh, you've been such pleasant company," said Miss Sally when the girls went away.

Mary took the little lady's hands in hers and looked affectionately down into her face.

"Would you like it—you and Juliana—if we came out to see you often? And perhaps brought some of our friends with us?"

"Oh, if you only would!" breathed Miss Sally.

Mary laughed and, obeying a sudden impulse, bent and kissed Miss Sally's cheek.

"We'll come then," she promised. "Please look upon us as your 'steady company' henceforth."

The girls kept their word. Thereafter, nearly every Saturday of the summer found them taking tea with Miss Sally at Golden Gate. Sometimes they came alone; sometimes they brought other girls. It soon became a decided "fad" in their set to go to see Miss Sally. Everybody who met her loved her at sight. It was considered a special treat to be taken by the Seymours to Golden Gate.

As for Miss Sally, her cup of happiness was almost full. She had "company" to her heart's content and of the very kind she loved—bright, merry, fun-loving girls who devoured her dainties with a frank zest that delighted her, filled the quaint old rooms with laughter and life, and chattered to her of all their plans and frolics and hopes. There was just one little cloud on Miss Sally's fair sky.

"If only Cousin Abner's girls would come!" she once said wistfully to Mary. "Nobody can quite take the place of one's own, you know. My heart yearns after them."

Mary was very silent and thoughtful as she drove back to Trenton that night. Two days afterwards, she went to Mrs. Gardiner's lawn party. The Reed girls were there. They were tall, fair, handsome girls, somewhat too lavishly and pronouncedly dressed in expensive gowns and hats, and looking, as they felt, very much on the outside of things. They brightened and bridled, however, when Mrs. Gardiner brought Mary Seymour up and introduced her. If there was one thing on earth that the Reed girls longed for more than another it was to "get in" with the Seymour girls.

After Mary had chatted with them for a few minutes in a friendly way, she said, "I think we have a mutual friend in Miss Sally Temple of Golden Gate, haven't we? I'm sure I've heard her speak of you."

The Reed girls flushed. They did not care to have the rich Seymour girls know of their connection with that queer old cousin of their father's who lived in that out-of-the-world spot up-country.

"She is a distant cousin of ours," said Beatrice carelessly, "but we've never met her."

"Oh, how much you have missed!" said Mary frankly. "She is the sweetest and most charming little lady I have ever met, and I am proud to number her among my friends. Golden Gate is such an idyllic little spot, too. We go there so often that I fear Miss Sally will think we mean to outwear our welcome. We hope to have her visit us in town this winter. Well, good-by for now. I'll tell Miss Sally I've met you. She will be pleased to hear about you."

When Mary had gone, the Reed girls looked at each other.

"I suppose we ought to have gone to see Cousin Sally before," said Beatrice. "Father said we ought to."

"How on earth did the Seymours pick her up?" said Helen. "Of course we must go and see her."

Go they did. The very next day Miss Sally's cup of happiness brimmed right over, for Cousin Abner's girls came to Golden Gate at last. They were very nice to her, too. Indeed, in spite of a good deal of snobbishness and false views of life, they were good-hearted girls under it all; and some plain common sense they had inherited from their father came to the surface and taught them to see that Miss Sally was a relative of whom anyone might be proud. They succumbed to her charm, as the others had done, and thoroughly enjoyed their visit to Golden Gate. They went away promising to come often again; and I may say right here that they kept their promise, and a real friendship grew up between Miss Sally and "Cousin Abner's girls" that was destined to work wonders for the latter, not only socially and mentally but spiritually as well, for it taught them that sincerity and honest kindliness of heart and manner are the best passports everywhere, and that pretence of any kind is a vulgarity not to be tolerated. This took time, of course. The Reed girls could not discard their snobbishness all at once. But in the end it was pretty well taken out of them.

Miss Sally never dreamed of this or the need for it. She loved Cousin Abner's girls from the first and always admired them exceedingly.

"And then it is so good to have your own folks coming as company," she told the Seymour girls. "Oh, I'm just in the seventh heaven of happiness. But, dearies, I think you will always be my favourites—mine and Juliana's. I've plenty of company now and it's all thanks to you."

"Oh, no," said Mary quickly. "Miss Sally, your company comes to you for just your own sake. You've made Golden Gate a veritable Mecca for us all. You don't know and you never will know how much good you have done us. You are so good and true and sweet that we girls all feel as if we were bound to live up to you, don't you see? And we all love you, Miss Sally."

"I'm so glad," breathed Miss Sally with shining eyes, "and so is Juliana."

Mrs. March's Revenge

"I declare, it is a real fall day," said Mrs. Stapp, dropping into a chair with a sigh of relief as Mrs. March ushered her into the cosy little sitting-room. "The wind would chill the marrow in your bones; winter'll be here before you know it."

"That's so," assented Mrs. March, bustling about to stir up the fire. "But I don't know as I mind it at all. Winter is real pleasant when it does come, but I must say, I don't fancy these betwixt-and-between days much. Sit up to the fire, Theodosia. You look real blue."

"I feel so too. Lawful heart, but this is comfort. This chimney-corner of yours, Anna, is the cosiest spot in the world."

"When did you get home from Maitland?" asked Mrs. March. "Did you have a pleasant time? And how did you leave Emily and the children?"

Mrs. Stapp took this trio of interrogations in calm detail.

"I came home Saturday," she said, as she unrolled her knitting. "Nice wet day it was too! And as for my visit, yes, I enjoyed myself pretty, well, not but what I worried over Peter's rheumatism a good deal. Emily is well, and the children ought to be, for such rampageous young ones I never saw! Emily can't do no more with them than an old hen with a brood of ducks. But, lawful heart, Anna, don't mind about my little affairs! The news Peter had for me about you when I got home fairly took my breath. He came down to the garden gate to shout it before I was out of the wagon. I couldn't believe but what he was joking at first. You should have seen Peter. He had an old red shawl tied round his rheumatic shoulder, and he was waving his arms like a crazy man. I declare, I thought the chimney was afire! Theodosia, Theodosia!' he shouted. 'Anna March has had a fortune left her by her brother in Australy, and she's bought the old Carroll place, and is going to move up there!' That was his salute when I got home. I'd have been over before this to hear all about it, but things were at such sixes and sevens in the house that I couldn't go visiting until I'd straightened them out a bit. Peter's real neat, as men go, but, lawful heart, such a mess as he makes of housekeeping! I didn't know you had a brother living."

"No more did I, Theodosia. I thought, as everyone else did, that poor Charles was at the bottom of the sea forty years ago. It's that long since he ran away from home. He had a quarrel with Father, and he was always dreadful high-spirited. He went to sea, and we heard that he had sailed for England in the *Helen Ray*. She was never heard of after, and we all supposed that my poor brother had perished with her. And four weeks ago I got a letter from a firm of lawyers in Melbourne, Australia, saying that my brother, Charles Bennett, had died and left all his fortune to me. I couldn't believe it at first, but they sent me some things of his that he had when he left home, and there was an old picture of myself among them with my name written on it in my own hand, so then I knew there was no mistake. But whether Charles did sail in the *Helen Ray*, or if he did, how he escaped from her and got to Australia, I don't know, and it isn't likely I ever will."

"Well, of all wonderful things!" commented Mrs. Stapp.

"I was glad to hear that I was heir to so much money," said Mrs. March firmly. "At first I felt as if it were awful of me to be glad when it came to me by my brother's death. But I mourned for poor Charles forty years ago, and I can't sense that he has only just died. Not but what I'd rather have seen him come home alive than have all the money in the world, but it has come about otherwise, and as the money is lawfully mine, I may as well feel pleased about it."

"And you've bought the Carroll place," said Mrs. Stapp, with the freedom of a privileged friend. "Whatever made you do it? I'm sure you are as cosy here as need be, and nobody but yourself. Isn't this house big enough for you?"

"No, it isn't. All my life I've been hankering for a good, big, roomy house, and all my life I've had to put up with little boxes of places, not big enough to turn round in. I've been contented, and made the best of what I had, but now that I can afford it, I mean to have a house that will suit me. The Carroll house is just what I want, for all it is a little old-fashioned. I've always had a notion of that house, although I never expected to own it any more than the moon."

"It's a real handsome place," admitted Mrs. Stapp, "but I expect it will need a lot of fixing up. Nobody has lived in it for six years. When are you going to move in?"

"In about three weeks, if all goes well. I'm having it all painted and done over inside. The outside can wait until the spring."

"It's queer how things come about," said Mrs. Stapp meditatively. "I guess old Mrs. Carroll never imagined her home was going to pass into other folks' hands as it has. When you and I were girls, and Louise Carroll was giving herself such airs over us, you didn't much expect to ever stand in her shoes, did you? Do you remember Lou?"

"Yes, I do," said Mrs. March sharply. A change came over her sonsy, smiling face. It actually looked hard and revengeful, and a cruel light flickered in her dark brown eyes. "I'll not forget Lou Carroll as long as I live. She is the only person in this world I ever hated. I suppose it is sinful to say it, but I hate her still, and always will."

"I never liked her myself," admitted Mrs. Stapp. "She thought herself above us all. Well, for that matter I suppose she was—but she needn't have rubbed it in so."

"Well, she might have been above me," said Mrs. March bitterly, "but she wasn't above twitting and snubbing me every chance she got. She always had a spite at me from the time we were children together at school. When we grew up it was worse. I couldn't begin to tell you all the times that girl insulted me. But there was once in particular—I'll never forgive her for it. I was at a party, and she was there too, and so was that young Trenham Manning, who was visiting the Ashleys. Do you remember him, Dosia? He was a handsome young fellow, and Lou had a liking for him, so all the girls said. But he never looked at her that night, and he kept by me the whole time. It made Lou furious, and at last she came up to me with a sneer on her face, and her black eyes just snapping, and said, 'Miss Bennett, Mother told me to tell you to tell your ma that if that plain sewing isn't done by tomorrow night she'll send for it and give it to somebody else; if people engage to have work done by a certain time and don't keep their word, they needn't expect to get it.' Oh, how badly I felt! Mother and I were poor, and had to work hard, but we had feelings just like other people, and to be insulted like that before Trenham Manning! I just burst out crying then and there, and ran away and hid. It was very silly of me, but I couldn't help it. That stings me yet. If I was ever to get a chance to pay Lou Carroll out for that, I'd take it without any compunction."

"Oh, but that is unchristian!" protested Mrs. Stapp feebly.

"Perhaps so, but it's the way I feel. Old Parson Jones used to say that people were marbled good and bad pretty even, but that in everybody there were one or two streaks just pure wicked. I guess Lou Carroll is my wicked streak. I haven't seen or heard of her for years—

ever since she married that worthless Dency Baxter and went away. She may be dead for all I know. I don't expect ever to have a chance to pay her out. But mark what I say, Theodosia, if I ever have, I will."

Mrs. March snipped off her thread, as if she challenged the world. Mrs. Stapp felt uncomfortable over the unusual display of feeling she had evoked, and hastened to change the subject.

In three weeks' time Mrs. March was established in her new home, and the "old Carroll house" blossomed out into renewed splendour. Theodosia Stapp, who had dropped in to see it, was in a rapture of admiration.

"You have a lovely home now, Anna. I used to think it fine enough in the Carrolls' time, but it wasn't as grand as this. And that reminds me, I have something to tell you, but I don't want you to get as excited as you did the last time I mentioned her name. You remember the last day I was to see you we were talking of Lou Carroll? Well, next day I was downtown in a store, and who should sail in but Mrs. Joel Kent, from Oriental. You know Mrs. Joel—Sarah Chapple that was? She and her man keep a little hotel up at Oriental. They're not very well off. She is a cousin of old Mrs. Carroll, but, lawful heart, the Carrolls didn't used to make much of the relationship! Well, Mrs. Joel and I had a chat. She told me all her troubles—she always has lots of them. Sarah was always of a grumbling turn, and she had a brand-new stock of them this time. What do you think, Anna March? Lou Carroll—or Mrs. Baxter, I suppose I should say—is up there at Joel Kent's at Oriental, dying of consumption; leastwise, Mrs. Joel says she is."

"Lou Carroll dying at Oriental!" cried Mrs. March.

"Yes. She came there from goodness knows where, about a month ago—might as well have dropped from the clouds, Mrs. Joel says, for all she expected of it. Her husband is dead, and I guess he led her a life of it when he was alive, and she's as poor as second skimmings. She was aiming to come here, Mrs. Joel says, but when she got to Oriental she wasn't fit to stir a step further, and the Kents had to keep her. I gather from what Mrs. Joel said that she's rather touched in her mind too, and has an awful hankering to get home here—to this very house. She appears to have the idea that it is hers, and all just the same as it used to be. I guess she is a sight of trouble, and Mrs. Joel ain't the woman to like that. But there! She has to work most awful hard, and I suppose a sick person doesn't come handy in a hotel. I guess you've got your revenge, Anna, without lifting a finger to get it. Think of Lou Carroll coming to that!"

The next day was cold and raw. The ragged, bare trees in the old Carroll grounds shook and writhed in the gusts of wind. Now and then a drifting scud of rain dashed across the windows. Mrs. March looked out with a shiver, and turned thankfully to her own cosy fireside again.

Presently she thought she heard a low knock at the front door, and went to see. As she opened it a savage swirl of damp wind rushed in, and the shrinking figure leaning against one of the fluted columns of the Grecian porch seemed to cower before its fury. It was a woman who stood there, a woman whose emaciated face wore a piteous expression, as she lifted it to Mrs. March.

"You don't know me, of course," she said, with a feeble attempt at dignity. "I am Mrs. Baxter. I—I used to live here long ago. I thought I'd walk over today and see my old home."

A fit of coughing interrupted her words, and she trembled like a leaf.

"Gracious me!" exclaimed Mrs. March blankly. "You don't mean to tell me that you have walked over from Oriental today—and you a sick woman! For pity's sake, come in, quick. And if you're not wet to the skin!"

She fairly pulled her visitor into the hall, and led her to the sitting-room.

"Sit down. Take this big easy-chair right up to the fire—so. Let me take your bonnet and shawl. I must run right out to tell Hannah to get you a hot drink."

"You are very kind," whispered the other. "I don't know you, but you look like a woman I used to know when I was a girl. She was a Mrs. Bennett, and she had a daughter, Anna. Do you know what became of her? I forget. I forget everything now."

"My name is March," said Mrs. March briefly, ignoring the question. "I don't suppose you ever heard it before."

She wrapped her own warm shawl about the other woman's thin shoulders. Then she hastened to the kitchen and soon returned, carrying a tray of food and a steaming hot drink. She wheeled a small table up to her visitor's side and said, very kindly,

"Now, take a bite, my dear, and this raspberry vinegar will warm you right up. It is a dreadful day for you to be out. Why on earth didn't Joel Kent drive you over?"

"They didn't know I was coming," whispered Mrs. Baxter anxiously. "I—I ran away. Sarah wouldn't have let me come if she had known. But I wanted to come so much. It is so nice to be home again."

Mrs. March watched her guest as she ate and drank. It was plain enough that her mind, or rather her memory, was affected. She did not realize that this was no longer her home. At moments she seemed to fancy herself back in the past again. Once or twice she called Mrs. March "Mother."

Presently a sharp knock was heard at the hall door. Mrs. March excused herself and went out. In the porch stood Theodosia Stapp and a woman whom Mrs. March did not at first glance recognize—a tall, aggressive-looking person, whose sharp black eyes darted in past Mrs. March and searched every corner of the hall before anyone had time to speak.

"Lawful heart!" puffed Mrs. Stapp, as she stepped in out of the biting wind. "I'm right out of breath. Mrs. March, allow me to introduce Mrs. Kent. We're looking for Mrs. Baxter. She has run away, and we thought perhaps she came here. Did she?"

"She is in my sitting-room now," said Mrs. March quietly.

"Didn't I say so?" demanded Mrs. Kent, turning to Mrs. Stapp. She spoke in a sharp, high-pitched tone that grated on Mrs. March's nerves. "Doesn't she beat all! She slipped away this morning when I was busy in the kitchen. And to think of her walking six miles over here in this wind! I dunno how she did it. I don't believe she's half as sick as she pretends. Well, I've got my wagon out here, Mrs. March, and I'll be much obliged if you'll tell her I'm here to take her home. I s'pose we'll have a fearful scene."

"I don't see that there is any call for a scene," said Mrs. March firmly. "The poor woman has just got here, and she thinks she has got home. She might as well think so if it is of any comfort to her. You'd better leave her here."

Theodosia gave a stifled gasp of amazement, but Mrs. March went serenely on.

"I'll take care of the poor soul as long as she needs it—and that will not be very long in my opinion, for if ever I saw death in a woman's face, it is looking out of hers. I've plenty of time to look after her and make her comfortable."

Mrs. Joel Kent was voluble in her thanks. It was evident that she was delighted to get the sick woman off her hands. Mrs. March cut her short with an invitation to stay to tea, but Mrs. Kent declined.

"I've got to hurry home straight off and get the men's suppers. Such a scamper to have over that woman! I'm sure I'm thankful you're willing to let her stay, for she'd never be contented anywhere else. I'll send over what few things she has tomorrow."

When Mrs. Kent had gone, Mrs. March and Mrs. Stapp looked at each other.

"And so this is your revenge, Anna March?" said the latter solemnly. "Do you remember what you said to me about her?"

"Yes, I do, Theodosia, and I thought I meant every word of it. But I guess my wicked streak ran out just when I needed it to depend on. Besides, you see, I've thought of Lou Carroll all these years as she was when I knew her—handsome and saucy and proud. But that poor creature in there isn't any more like the Lou Carroll I knew than you are—not a mite. The old Lou Carroll is dead already, and my spite is dead with her. Will you come in and see her?"

"Well, no, not just now. She wouldn't know me, and Mrs. Joel says strangers kind of excite her—a pretty bad place the hotel would be for her at that rate, I should think. I must go and tell Peter about it, and I'll send up some of my black currant jam for her."

When Mrs. Stapp had gone, Mrs. March went back to her guest. Lou Baxter had fallen asleep with her head pillowed on the soft plush back of her chair. Mrs. March looked at the hollow, hectic cheeks and the changed, wasted features, and her bright brown eyes softened with tears.

"Poor Lou," she said softly, as she brushed a loose lock of grey hair back from the sleeping woman's brow.

Nan

Nan was polishing the tumblers at the pantry window, outside of which John Osborne was leaning among the vines. His arms were folded on the sill and his straw hat was pushed back from his flushed, eager face as he watched Nan's deft movements.

Beyond them, old Abe Stewart was mowing the grass in the orchard with a scythe and casting uneasy glances at the pair. Old Abe did not approve of John Osborne as a suitor for Nan. John was poor; and old Abe, although he was the wealthiest farmer in Granville, was bent on Nan's making a good match. He looked upon John Osborne as a mere fortune-hunter, and it was a thorn in the flesh to see him talking to Nan while he, old Abe, was too far away to hear what they were saying. He had a good deal of confidence in Nan, she was a sensible, level-headed girl. Still, there was no knowing what freak even a sensible girl might take into her head, and Nan was so determined when she did make up her mind. She was his own daughter in that.

However, old Abe need not have worried himself. It could not be said that Nan was helping John Osborne on in his wooing at all. Instead, she was teasing and snubbing him by turns.

Nan was very pretty. Moreover, Nan was well aware of the fact. She knew that the way her dark hair curled around her ears and forehead was bewitching; that her complexion was the envy of every girl in Granville; that her long lashes had a trick of drooping over very soft, dark eyes in a fashion calculated to turn masculine heads hopelessly. John Osborne knew all this too, to his cost. He had called to ask Nan to go with him to the Lone Lake picnic the next day. At this request Nan dropped her eyes and murmured that she was sorry, but he was too late—she had promised to go with somebody else. There was no need of Nan's making such a mystery about it. The somebody else was her only cousin, Ned Bennett, who had had a quarrel with his own girl; the latter lived at Lone Lake, and Ned had coaxed Nan to go over with him and try her hand at patching matters up between him and his offended lady-love. And Nan, who was an amiable creature and tender-hearted where anybody's lover except her own was concerned, had agreed to go.

But John Osborne at once jumped to the conclusion—as Nan had very possibly meant him to do—that the mysterious somebody was Bryan Lee, and the thought was gall and wormwood to him.

"Whom are you going with?" he asked.

"That would be telling," Nan said, with maddening indifference.

"Is it Bryan Lee?" demanded John.

"It might be," said Nan reflectively, "and then again, you know, it mightn't."

John was silent; he was no match for Nan when it came to a war of words. He scowled moodily at the shining tumblers.

"Nan, I'm going out west," he said finally.

Nan stared at him with her last tumbler poised in mid-air, very much as if he had announced his intention of going to the North Pole or Equatorial Africa.

"John Osborne, are you crazy?"

"Not quite. And I'm in earnest, I can tell you that."

Nan set the glass down with a decided thud. John's curtness displeased her. He needn't suppose that it made any difference to her if he took it into his stupid head to go to Afghanistan.

"Oh!" she remarked carelessly. "Well, I suppose if you've got the Western fever your case is hopeless. Would it be impertinent to inquire why you are going?"

"There's nothing else for me to do, Nan," said John, "Bryan Lee is going to foreclose the mortgage next month and I'll have to clear out. He says he can't wait any longer. I've worked hard enough and done my best to keep the old place, but it's been uphill work and I'm beaten at last."

Nan sat blankly down on the stool by the window. Her face was a study which John Osborne, watching old Abe's movements, missed.

"Well, I never!" she gasped. "John Osborne, do you mean to tell me that Bryan Lee is going to do that? How did he come to get your mortgage?"

"Bought it from old Townsend," answered John briefly. "Oh, he's within his rights, I'll admit. I've even got behind with the interest this past year. I'll go out west and begin over again."

"It's a burning shame!" said Nan violently.

John looked around in time to see two very red spots on her cheeks.

"You don't care though, Nan."

"I don't like to see anyone unjustly treated," declared Nan, "and that is what you've been. You've never had half a chance. And after the way you've slaved, too!"

"If Lee would wait a little I might do something yet, now that Aunt Alice is gone," said John bitterly. "I'm not afraid of work. But he won't; he means to take his spite out at last."

Nan hesitated.

"Surely Bryan isn't so mean as that," she stammered. "Perhaps he'll change his mind if—if—"

Osborne wheeled about with face aflame.

"Don't you say a word to him about it, Nan!" he cried. "Don't you go interceding with him for me. I've got some pride left. He can take the farm from me, and he can take you maybe, but he can't take my self-respect. I won't beg him for mercy. Don't you dare to say a word to him about it."

Nan's eyes flashed. She was offended to find her sympathy flung back in her face.

"Don't be alarmed," she said tartly. "I shan't bother myself about your concerns. I've no doubt you're able to look out for them yourself."

Osborne turned away. As he did so he saw Bryan Lee driving up the lane. Perhaps Nan saw it too. At any rate, she leaned out of the window.

"John! John!" Osborne half turned. "You'll be up again soon, won't you?"

His face hardened. "I'll come to say goodbye before I go, of course," he answered shortly.

He came face to face with Lee at the gate, where the latter was tying his sleek chestnut to a poplar. He acknowledged his rival's condescending nod with a scowl. Lee looked after him with a satisfied smile.

"Poor beggar!" he muttered. "He feels pretty cheap I reckon. I've spoiled his chances in this quarter. Old Abe doesn't want any poverty-stricken hangers-on about his place and Nan won't dream of taking him when she knows he hasn't a roof over his head."

He stopped for a chat with old Abe. Old Abe approved of Bryan Lee. He was a son-in-law after old Abe's heart.

Meanwhile, Nan had seated herself at the pantry window and was ostentatiously hemming towels in apparent oblivion of suitor No. 2. Nevertheless, when Bryan came up she greeted him with an unusually sweet smile and at once plunged into an animated conversation. Bryan had not come to ask her to go to the picnic—business prevented him from going. But he meant to find out if she were going with John Osborne. As Nan was serenely impervious to all hints, he was finally forced to ask her bluntly if she was going to the picnic.

Well, yes, she expected to.

Oh! Might he ask with whom?

Nan didn't know that it was a question of public interest at all.

"It isn't with that Osborne fellow, is it?" demanded Bryan incautiously.

Nan tossed her head. "Well, why not?" she asked.

"Look here, Nan," said Lee angrily, "if you're going to the picnic with John Osborne I'm surprised at you. What do you mean by encouraging him so? He's as poor as Job's turkey. I suppose you've heard that I've been compelled to foreclose the mortgage on his farm."

Nan kept her temper sweetly—a dangerous sign, had Bryan but known it.

"Yes; he was telling me so this morning," she answered slowly.

"Oh, was he? I suppose he gave me my character?"

"No; he didn't say very much about it at all. He said of course you were within your rights. But do you really mean to do it, Bryan?"

"Of course I do," said Bryan promptly. "I can't wait any longer for my money, and I'd never get it if I did. Osborne can't even pay the interest."

"It isn't because he hasn't worked hard enough, then," said Nan. "He has just slaved on that place ever since he grew up."

"Well, yes, he has worked hard in a way. But he's kind of shiftless, for all that—no manager, as you might say. Some folks would have been clear by now, but Osborne is one of those men that are bound to get behind. He hasn't got any business faculty."

"He isn't shiftless," said Nan quickly, "and it isn't his fault if he has got behind. It's all because of his care for his aunt. He has had to spend more on her doctor's bills than would have raised the mortgage. And now that she is dead and he might have a chance to pull up, you go and foreclose."

"A man must look out for Number One," said Bryan easily, admiring Nan's downcast eyes and rosy cheeks. "I haven't any spite against Osborne, but business is business, you know."

Nan opened her lips to say something but, remembering Osborne's parting injunction, she shut them again. She shot a scornful glance at Lee as he stood with his arms folded on the sill beside her.

Bryan lingered, talking small talk, until Nan announced that she must see about getting tea.

"And you won't tell me who is going to take you to the picnic?" he coaxed.

"Oh, it's Ned Bennett," said Nan indifferently.

Bryan felt relieved. He unpinned the huge cluster of violets on his coat and laid them down on the sill beside her before he went. Nan flicked them off with her fingers as she watched him cross the lawn, his own self-satisfied smile upon his face.

A week later the Osborne homestead had passed into Bryan Lee's hands and John Osborne was staying with his cousin at Thornhope, pending his departure for the west. He had never been to see Nan since that last afternoon, but Bryan Lee haunted the Stewart place. One day he suddenly stopped coming and, although Nan was discreetly silent, in due time it came to old Abe's ears by various driblets of gossip that Nan had refused him.

Old Abe marched straightway home to Nan in a fury and demanded if this were true. Nan curtly admitted that it was. Old Abe was so much taken aback by her coolness that he asked almost meekly what was her reason for doing such a fool trick.

"Because he turned John Osborne out of house and home," returned Nan composedly. "If he hadn't done that there is no telling what might have happened. I might even have married him, because I liked him very well and it would have pleased you. At any rate, I wouldn't have married John when you were against him. Now I mean to."

Old Abe stormed furiously at this, but Nan kept so provokingly cool that he was conscious of wasting breath. He went off in a rage, but Nan did not feel particularly anxious now that the announcement was over. He would cool down, she knew. John Osborne worried her more. She didn't see clearly how she was to marry him unless he asked her, and he had studiously avoided her since the foreclosure.

But Nan did not mean to be baffled or to let her lover slip through her fingers for want of a little courage. She was not old Abe Stewart's daughter for nothing.

One day Ned Bennett dropped in and said that John Osborne would start for the west in three days. That evening Nan went up to her room and dressed herself in the prettiest dress she owned, combed her hair around her sparkling face in bewitching curls, pinned a cluster of apple blossoms at her belt, and, thus equipped, marched down in the golden sunset light to the Mill Creek Bridge. John Osborne, on his return from

Thornhope half an hour later, found her there, leaning over the rail among the willows.

Nan started in well-assumed surprise and then asked him why he had not been to see her. John blushed—stammered—didn't know—had been busy. Nan cut short his halting excuses by demanding to know if he were really going away, and what he intended to do.

"I'll go out on the prairies and take up a claim," said Osborne sturdily. "Begin life over again free of debt. It'll be hard work, but I'm not afraid of that. I will succeed if it takes me years."

They walked on in silence. Nan came to the conclusion that Osborne meant to hold his peace.

"John," she said tremulously, "won't—won't you find it very lonely out there?"

"Of course—I expect that. I shall have to get used to it."

Nan grew nervous. Proposing to a man was really very dreadful.

"Wouldn't it be—nicer for you"—she faltered—"that is—it wouldn't be so lonely for you—would it—if—if you had me out there with you?"

John Osborne stopped squarely in the dusty road and looked at her. "Nan!" he exclaimed.

"Oh, if you can't take a hint!" said Nan in despair.

It was all of an hour later that a man drove past them as they loitered up the hill road in the twilight. It was Bryan Lee; he had taken from Osborne his house and land, but he had not been able to take Nan Stewart, after all.

Natty of Blue Point

Natty Miller strolled down to the wharf where Bliss Ford was tying up the *Cockawee*. Bliss was scowling darkly at the boat, a trim new one, painted white, whose furled sails seemed unaccountably wet and whose glistening interior likewise dripped with moisture. A group of fishermen on the wharf were shaking their heads sagely as Natty drew near.

"Might as well split her up for kindlings, Bliss," said Jake McLaren. "You'll never get men to sail in her. It passed the first time, seeing as only young Johnson was skipper, but when a boat turns turtle with Captain Frank in command, there's something serious wrong with her."

"What's up?" asked Natty.

"The *Cockawee* upset out in the bay again this morning," answered Will Scott. "That's the second time. The *Grey Gull* picked up the men and towed her in. It's no use trying to sail her. Lobstermen ain't going to risk their lives in a boat like that. How's things over at Blue Point, Natty?"

"Pretty well," responded Natty laconically. Natty never wasted words. He had not talked a great deal in his fourteen years of life, but he was much given to thinking. He was rather undersized and insignificant looking, but there were a few boys of his own age on the mainland who knew that Natty had muscles.

"Has Everett heard anything from Ottawa about the lighthouse business yet?" asked Will.

Natty shook his head.

"Think he's any chance of getting the app'intment?" queried Adam Lewis.

"Not the ghost of a chance," said Cooper Creasy decidedly. "He's on the wrong side of politics, that's what. Er rather his father was. A

Tory's son ain't going to get an app'intment from a Lib'ral government, that's what."

"Mr. Barr says that Everett is too young to be trusted in such a responsible position," quoted Natty gravely.

Cooper shrugged his shoulders.

"Mebbe—mebbe. Eighteen is kind of green, but everybody knows that Ev's been the real lighthouse keeper for two years, since your father took sick. Irving Elliott wants that light—has wanted it for years—and he's a pretty strong pull at headquarters, that's what. Barr owes him something for years of hard work at elections. I ain't saying anything against Elliott, either. He's a good man, but your father's son ought to have that light as sure as he won't get it, that's what."

"Any of you going to take in the sports tomorrow down at Summerside?" asked Will Scott, in order to switch Cooper away from politics, which were apt to excite him.

"I'm going, for one," said Adam. "There's to be a yacht race atween the Summerside and Charlottetown boat clubs. Yes, I am going. Give you a chance down to the station, Natty, if you want one."

Natty shook his head.

"Not going," he said briefly.

"You should celebrate Victoria Day," said Adam, patriotically. "'Twenty-fourth o' May's the Queen's birthday, Ef we don't get a holiday we'll all run away,' as we used to say at school. The good old Queen is dead, but the day's been app'inted a national holiday in honour of her memory and you should celebrate it becoming, Natty-boy."

"Ev and I can't both go, and he's going," explained Natty. "Prue and I'll stay home to light up. Must be getting back now. Looks squally."

"I misdoubt if we'll have Queen's weather tomorrow," said Cooper, squinting critically at the sky. "Looks like a northeast blow, that's what. There goes Bliss, striding off and looking pretty mad. The *Cockawee's* a dead loss to him, that's what. Nat's off—he knows how to handle a boat middling well, too. Pity he's such a puny youngster. Not much to him, I reckon."

Natty had cast loose in his boat, the *Merry Maid*, and hoisted his sail. In a few minutes he was skimming gaily down the bay. The wind was fair and piping and the *Merry Maid* went like a bird. Natty, at the rudder, steered for Blue Point Island, a reflective frown on his face. He was feeling in no mood for Victoria Day sports. In a very short time he and Ev and Prue must leave Blue Point lighthouse, where they had lived all their lives. To Natty it seemed as if the end of all things would come then. Where would life be worth living away from lonely, windy Blue Point Island?

David Miller had died the preceding winter after a long illness. He had been lighthouse keeper at Blue Point for thirty years. His three children had been born and brought up there, and there, four years ago, the mother had died. But womanly little Prue had taken her place well, and the boys were devoted to their sister. When their father died, Everett had applied for the position of lighthouse keeper. The matter was not yet publicly decided, but old Cooper Creasy had sized the situation up accurately. The Millers had no real hope that Everett would be appointed.

Victoria Day, while not absolutely stormy, proved to be rather unpleasant. A choppy northeast wind blew up the bay, and the water was rough enough. The sky was overcast with clouds, and the May air was raw and chilly. At Blue Point the Millers were early astir, for if Everett wanted to sail over to the mainland in time to catch the excursion train, no morning naps were permissible. He was going alone. Since only one of the boys could go, Natty had insisted that it should be Everett, and Prue had elected to stay home with Natty. Prue had small heart for Victoria Day that year. She did not feel even a thrill of enthusiasm when Natty hoisted a flag and wreathed the Queen's picture with creeping spruce. Prue felt as badly about leaving Blue Point Island as the boys did.

The day passed slowly. In the afternoon the wind fell away to a dead calm, but there was still a heavy swell on, and shortly before sunset a fog came creeping up from the east and spread over the bay and islands, so thick and white that Prue and Natty could not even see Little Bear Island on the right.

"I'm glad Everett isn't coming back tonight," said Prue. "He could never find his way cross the harbour in that fog."

"Isn't it thick, though," said Natty. "The light won't show far tonight."

At sunset they lighted the great lamps and then settled down to an evening of reading. But it was not long before Natty looked up from his book to say, "Hello, Prue, what was that? Thought I heard a noise."

"So did I," said Prue. "I sounded like someone calling."

They hurried to the door, which looked out on the harbour. The night, owing to the fog, was dark with a darkness that seemed almost tangible. From somewhere out of that darkness came a muffled shouting, like that of a person in distress.

"Prue, there's somebody in trouble out there!" exclaimed Natty.

"Oh, it's surely never Ev!" cried Prue.

Natty shook his head.

"Don't think so. Ev had no intention of coming back tonight. Get that lantern, Prue. I must go and see what and who it is."

"Oh, Natty, you mustn't," cried Prue in distress. "There's a heavy swell on yet—and the fog—oh, if you get lost—"

"I'll not get lost, and I must go, Prue. Maybe somebody is drowning out there. It's not Ev, of course, but suppose it were! That's a good girl."

Prue, with set face, had brought the lantern, resolutely choking back the words of fear and protest that rushed to her lips. They hurried down to the shore and Natty sprang into the little skiff he used for rowing. He hastily lashed the lantern in the stern, cast loose the painter, and lifted the oars.

"I'll be back as soon as possible," he called to Prue. "Wait here for me."

In a minute the shore was out of sight, and Natty found himself alone in the black fog, with no guide but the cries for help, which already were becoming fainter. They seemed to come from the direction of Little Bear, and thither Natty rowed. It was a tough pull, and the water was rough enough for the little dory. But Natty had been at home with the oars from babyhood, and his long training and tough sinews stood him in good stead now. Steadily and intrepidly he rowed along. The water grew rougher as he passed out from the shelter of Blue Point into the channel between the latter and Little Bear. The cries were becoming very faint. What if he should be too late? He bent to the oars with all his energy. Presently, by the smoother water, he knew he must be in the lea of Little Bear. The cries sounded nearer. He must already have rowed nearly a mile. The next minute he shot around a small headland and right before him, dimly visible in the faint light cast by the lantern through the fog, was an upturned boat with two men clinging to it, one on each side, evidently almost exhausted. Natty rowed cautiously up to the one nearest him, knowing that he must be wary lest the grip of the drowning man overturn his own light skiff.

"Let go when I say," he shouted, "and don't—grab—anything, do you hear? Don't—grab. Now, let go."

The next minute the man lay in the dory, dragged over the stern by Netty's grip on his collar.

"Lie still," ordered Natty, clutching the oars. To row around the overturned boat, amid the swirl of water about her, was a task that taxed Netty's skill and strength to the utmost. The other man was dragged in over the bow, and with a gasp of relief Natty pulled away from the sinking boat. Once clear of her he could not row for a few minutes; he was shaking from head to foot with the reaction from tremendous effort and strain.

"This'll never do," he muttered. "I'm not going to be a baby now. But will I ever be able to row back?"

Presently, however, he was able to grip his oars again and pull for the lighthouse, whose beacon loomed dimly through the fog like a great blur of whiter mist. The men, obedient to his orders, lay quietly where he had placed them, and before long Natty was back again at the lighthouse landing, where Prue was waiting, wild with anxiety. The men were helped out and assisted up to the lighthouse, where Natty went to hunt up dry clothes for them, and Prue flew about to prepare hot drinks.

"To think that that child saved us!" exclaimed one of the men. "Why, I didn't think a grown man had the strength to do what he did. He is your brother, I suppose, Miss Miller. You have another brother, I think?"

"Oh, yes—Everett—but he is away," explained Prue. "We heard your shouts and Natty insisted on going at once to your rescue."

"Well, he came just in time. I couldn't have held on another minute—was so done up I couldn't have moved or spoken all the way here even if he hadn't commanded me to keep perfectly still."

Natty returned at this moment and exclaimed, "Why, it is Mr. Barr. I didn't recognize you before."

"Barr it is, young man. This gentleman is my friend, Mr. Blackmore. We have been celebrating Victoria Day by a shooting tramp over Little Bear. We hired a boat from Ford at the Harbour Head this morning—the *Cockawee*, he called her—and sailed over. I don't know much about running a boat, but Blackmore here thinks he does. We were at the other side of the island when the fog came up. We hurried across it, but it was almost dark when we reached our boat. We sailed around the point and then the boat just simply upset—don't know why—"

"But I know why," interrupted Natty indignantly. "That *Cockawee* does nothing but upset. She has turned turtle twice out in the harbour in fine weather. Ford was a rascal to let her to you. He might have known what would happen. Why—why—it was almost murder to let you go!"

"I thought there must be something queer about her," declared Mr. Blackmore. "I do know how to handle a boat despite my friend's gibe, and there was no reason why she should have upset like that. That Ford ought to be horsewhipped."

Thanks to Prue's stinging hot decoctions of black currant drink, the two gentlemen were no worse for their drenching and exposure, and the next morning Natty took them to the mainland in the *Merry Maid*. When he parted with them, Mr. Barr shook his hand heartily and said: "Thank you, my boy. You're a plucky youngster and a skilful one, too. Tell your brother that if I can get the Blue Point lighthouse berth for him I will, and as for yourself, you will always find a friend in me, and if I can ever do anything for you I will."

Two weeks later Everett received an official document formally appointing him keeper of Blue Point Island light. Natty carried the news to the mainland, where it was joyfully received among the fishermen.

"Only right and fair," said Cooper Creasy. "Blue Point without a Miller to light up wouldn't seem the thing at all, that's what. And it's nothing but Ev's doo."

"Guess Natty had more to do with it than Ev," said Adam, perpetrating a very poor pun and being immensely applauded therefor. It keyed Will Scott up to rival Adam.

"You said that Irving had a pull and the Millers hadn't," he said jocularly. "But it looks as if 'twas Natty's pull did the business after all—his pull over to Bear Island and back."

"It was about a miracle that a boy could do what he did on such a night," said Charles Macey.

"Where's Ford?" asked Natty uncomfortably. He hated to have his exploit talked about.

"Ford has cleared out," said Cooper, "gone down to Summerside to go into Tobe Meekins's factory there. Best thing he could do, that's what. Folks here hadn't no use for him after letting that death trap to them two men—even if they was Lib'rals. The *Cockawee* druv ashore on Little Bear, and there she's going to remain, I guess. D'ye want a berth in my mackerel boat this summer, Natty?"

"I do," said Natty, "but I thought you said you were full."

"I guess I can make room for you," said Cooper. "A boy with such grit and muscle ain't to be allowed to go to seed on Blue Point, that's what. Yesser, we'll make room for you."

And Natty's cup of happiness was full.

Penelope's Party Waist

"It's perfectly horrid to be so poor," grumbled Penelope. Penelope did not often grumble, but just now, as she sat tapping with one pink-tipped finger her invitation to Blanche Anderson's party, she felt that grumbling was the only relief she had.

Penelope was seventeen, and when one is seventeen and cannot go to a party because one hasn't a suitable dress to wear, the world is very apt to seem a howling wilderness.

"I wish I could think of some way to get you a new waist," said Doris, with what these sisters called "the poverty pucker" coming in the centre of her pretty forehead. "If your black skirt were sponged and pressed and re-hung, it would do very well."

Penelope saw the poverty pucker and immediately repented with all her impetuous heart having grumbled. That pucker came often enough without being brought there by extra worries.

"Well, there is no use sitting here sighing for the unattainable," she said, jumping up briskly. "I'd better be putting my grey matter into that algebra instead of wasting it plotting for a party dress that I certainly can't get. It's a sad thing for a body to lack brains when she wants to be a teacher, isn't it? If I could only absorb algebra and history as I can music, what a blessing it would be! Come now, Dorrie dear, smooth that pucker out. Next year I shall be earning a princely salary, which we can squander on party gowns at will—if people haven't given up inviting us by that time, in sheer despair of ever being able to conquer our exclusiveness."

Penelope went off to her detested algebra with a laugh, but the pucker did not go out of Doris' forehead. She wanted Penelope to go to that party.

Penelope has studied so hard all winter and she hasn't gone anywhere, thought the older sister wistfully. She is getting discouraged over those examinations and she needs just a good, jolly time to hearten her up. If it could only be managed!

But Doris did not see how it could. It took every cent of her small salary as typewriter in an uptown office to run their tiny establishment and keep Penelope in school dresses and books. Indeed, she could not have done even that much if they had not owned their little cottage. Next year it would be easier if Penelope got through her examinations successfully, but just now there was absolutely not a spare penny.

"It is hard to be poor. We are a pair of misfits," said Doris, with a patient little smile, thinking of Penelope's uncultivated talent for music and her own housewifely gifts, which had small chance of flowering out in her business life.

Doris dreamed of pretty dresses all that night and thought about them all the next day. So, it must be confessed, did Penelope, though she would not have admitted it for the world.

When Doris reached home the next evening, she found Penelope hovering over a bulky parcel on the sitting-room table.

"I'm so glad you've come," she said with an exaggerated gasp of relief. "I really don't think my curiosity could have borne the strain for another five minutes. The expressman brought this parcel an hour ago, and there's a letter for you from Aunt Adella on the clock shelf, and I think they belong to each other. Hurry up and find out. Dorrie, darling, what if it should be a—a—present of some sort or other!"

"I suppose it can't be anything else," smiled Doris. She knew that Penelope had started out to say "a new dress." She cut the strings and removed the wrappings. Both girls stared.

"Is it—it isn't—yes, it is! Doris Hunter, I believe it's an old quilt!"

Doris unfolded the odd present with a queer feeling of disappointment. She did not know just what she had expected the package to contain, but certainly not this. She laughed a little shakily.

"Well, we can't say after this that Aunt Adella never gave us anything," she said, when she had opened her letter. "Listen, Penelope."

My Dear Doris:

I have decided to give up housekeeping and go out West to live with Robert. So I am disposing of such of the family heirlooms as I do not wish to take with me. I am sending you by express your Grandmother Hunter's silk quilt. It is a handsome article still and I hope you will prize it as you should. It took your grandmother five years to make it. There is a bit of the wedding dress of every member of the family in it. Love to Penelope and yourself.

Your affectionate aunt,

Adella Hunter.

"I don't see its beauty," said Penelope with a grimace. "It may have been pretty once, but it is all faded now. It is a monument of patience, though. The pattern is what they call 'Little Thousands,' isn't it? Tell me, Dorrie, does it argue a lack of proper respect for my ancestors that I can't feel very enthusiastic over this heirloom—especially when Grandmother Hunter died years before I was born?"

"It was very kind of Aunt Adella to send it," said Doris dutifully.

"Oh, very," agreed Penelope drolly. "Only don't ever ask me to sleep under it. It would give me the nightmare. O-o-h!"

This last was a little squeal of admiration as Doris turned the quilt over and brought to view the shimmering lining.

"Why, the wrong side is ever so much prettier than the right!" exclaimed Penelope. "What lovely, old-timey stuff! And not a bit faded."

The lining was certainly very pretty. It was a soft, creamy yellow silk, with a design of brocaded pink rosebuds all over it.

"That was a dress Grandmother Hunter had when she was a girl," said Doris absently. "I remember hearing Aunt Adella speak of it. When it became old-fashioned, Grandmother used it to line her quilt. I declare, it is as good as new."

"Well, let us go and have tea," said Penelope. "I'm decidedly hungry. Besides, I see the poverty pucker coming. Put the quilt in the spare room. It is something to possess an heirloom, after all. It gives one a nice, important-family feeling."

After tea, when Penelope was patiently grinding away at her studies and thinking dolefully enough of the near-approaching examinations, which she dreaded, and of teaching, which she confidently expected to hate, Doris went up to the tiny spare room to look at the wrong side of the quilt again.

"It would make the loveliest party waist," she said under her breath. "Creamy yellow is Penelope's colour, and I could use that bit of old black lace and those knots of velvet ribbon that I have to trim it. I wonder if Grandmother Hunter's reproachful spirit will forever haunt me if I do it."

Doris knew very well that she would do it—had known it ever since she had looked at that lovely lining and a vision of Penelope's vivid face and red-brown hair rising above a waist of the quaint old silk had flashed before her mental sight. That night, after Penelope had gone to bed, Doris ripped the lining out of Grandmother Hunter's silk quilt.

"If Aunt Adella saw me now!" she laughed softly to herself as she worked.

In the three following evenings Doris made the waist. She thought it a wonderful bit of good luck that Penelope went out each of the evenings to study some especially difficult problems with a school chum.

"It will be such a nice surprise for her," the sister mused jubilantly.

Penelope was surprised as much as the tender, sisterly heart could wish when Doris flashed out upon her triumphantly on the evening of the party with the black skirt nicely pressed and re-hung, and the prettiest waist imaginable—a waist that was a positive "creation" of dainty rose-besprinkled silk, with a girdle and knots of black velvet.

"Doris Hunter, you are a veritable little witch! Do you mean to tell me that you conjured that perfectly lovely thing for me out of the lining of Grandmother Hunter's quilt?"

So Penelope went to Blanche's party and her dress was the admiration of every girl there. Mrs. Fairweather, who was visiting Mrs. Anderson, looked closely at it also. She was a very sweet old lady, with silver hair, which she wore in delightful, old-fashioned puffs, and she had very bright, dark eyes. Penelope thought her altogether charming.

"She looks as if she had just stepped out of the frame of some lovely old picture," she said to herself. "I wish she belonged to me. I'd just love to have a grandmother like her. And I do wonder who it is I've seen who looks so much like her."

A little later on the knowledge came to her suddenly, and she thought with inward surprise: Why, it is Doris, of course. If my sister Doris lives to be seventy years old and wears her hair in pretty white puffs, she will look exactly as Mrs. Fairweather does now.

Mrs. Fairweather asked to have Penelope introduced to her, and when they found themselves alone together she said gently, "My dear, I am going to ask a very impertinent question. Will you tell me where you got the silk of which your waist is made?"

Poor Penelope's pretty young face turned crimson. She was not troubled with false pride by any means, but she simply could not bring herself to tell Mrs. Fairweather that her waist was made out of the lining of an old heirloom quilt.

"My Aunt Adella gave me—gave us—the material," she stammered. "And my elder sister Doris made the waist for me. I think the silk once belonged to my Grandmother Hunter."

"What was your grandmother's maiden name?" asked Mrs. Fairweather eagerly.

"Penelope Saverne. I am named after her."

Mrs. Fairweather suddenly put her arm about Penelope and drew the young girl to her, her lovely old face aglow with delight and tenderness.

"Then you are my grandniece," she said. "Your grandmother was my half-sister. When I saw your dress, I felt sure you were related to her. I should recognize that rosebud silk if I came across it in Thibet. Penelope Saverne was the daughter of my mother by her first husband. Penelope was four years older than I was, but we were devoted to each other. Oddly enough, our birthdays fell on the same day, and when Penelope was twenty and I sixteen, my father gave us each a silk dress of this very material. I have mine yet.

"Soon after this our mother died and our household was broken up. Penelope went to live with her aunt and I went West with Father. This was long ago, you know, when travelling and correspondence were not the easy, matter-of-course things they are now. After a few years I lost touch with my half-sister. I married out West and have lived there all my life. I never knew what had become of Penelope. But tonight, when I saw you come in in that waist made of the rosebud silk, the whole past rose before me and I felt like a girl again. My dear, I am a very lonely old woman, with nobody belonging to me. You don't know how delighted I am to find that I have two grandnieces."

Penelope had listened silently, like a girl in a dream. Now she patted Mrs. Fairweather's soft old hand affectionately.

"It sounds like a storybook," she said gaily. "You must come and see Doris. She is such a darling sister. I wouldn't have had this waist if it hadn't been for her. I will tell you the whole truth—I don't mind it now. Doris made my party waist for me out of the lining of an old silk quilt of Grandmother Hunter's that Aunt Adella sent us."

Mrs. Fairweather did go to see Doris the very next day, and quite wonderful things came to pass from that interview. Doris and Penelope found their lives and plans changed in the twinkling of an eye. They were both to go and live with Aunt Esther—as Mrs. Fairweather had said they must call her. Penelope was to have, at last, her longed-for musical education and Doris was to be the home girl.

"You must take the place of my own dear little granddaughter," said Aunt Esther. "She died six years ago, and I have been so lonely since."

When Mrs. Fairweather had gone, Doris and Penelope looked at each other.

"Pinch me, please," said Penelope. "I'm half afraid I'll wake up and find I have been dreaming. Isn't it all wonderful, Doris Hunter?"

Doris nodded radiantly.

"Oh, Penelope, think of it! Music for you—somebody to pet and fuss over for me—and such a dear, sweet aunty for us both!"

"And no more contriving party waists out of old silk linings," laughed Penelope. "But it was very fortunate that you did it for once, sister mine. And no more poverty puckers," she concluded.

The Girl and The Wild Race

"If Judith would only get married," Mrs. Theodora Whitney was wont to sigh dolorously.

Now, there was no valid reason why Judith ought to get married unless she wanted to. But Judith was twenty-seven and Mrs. Theodora thought it was a terrible disgrace to be an old maid.

"There has never been an old maid in our family so far back as we know of," she lamented. "And to think that there should be one now! It just drags us down to the level of the McGregors. They have always been noted for their old maids."

Judith took all her aunt's lamentations good-naturedly. Sometimes she argued the subject placidly.

"Why are you in such a hurry to be rid of me, Aunt Theo? I'm sure we're very comfortable here together and you know you would miss me terribly if I went away."

"If you took the right one you wouldn't go so very far," said Mrs. Theodora, darkly significant. "And, anyhow, I'd put up with any amount of lonesomeness rather than have an old maid in the family. It's all very fine now, when you're still young enough and good looking, with lots of beaus at your beck and call. But that won't last much longer and if you go on with your dilly-dallying you'll wake up some fine day to find that your time for choosing has gone by. Your mother used to be dreadful proud of your good looks when you was a baby. I told her she needn't be. Nine times out of ten a beauty don't marry as well as an ordinary girl."

"I'm not much set on marrying at all," declared Judith sharply. Any reference to the "right one" always disturbed her placidity. The real root of the trouble was that Mrs. Theodora's "right one" and Judith's "right one" were two different people.

The Ramble Valley young men were very fond of dancing attendance on Judith, even if she were verging on old maidenhood. Her prettiness was undeniable; the Stewarts came to maturity late and at twenty-seven Judith's dower of milky-white flesh, dimpled red lips and shining bronze hair was at its fullest splendor. Besides, she was "jolly," and jollity went a long way in Ramble Valley popularity.

Of all Judith's admirers Eben King alone found favor in Mrs. Theodora's eyes. He owned the adjoining farm, was well off and homely—so homely that Judith declared it made her eyes ache to look at him.

Bruce Marshall, Judith's "right one" was handsome, but Mrs. Theodora looked upon him with sour disapproval. He owned a stony little farm at the remote end of Ramble Valley and was reputed to be fonder of many things than of work. To be sure, Judith had enough capability and energy for two; but Mrs. Theodora detested a lazy man. She ordered Judith not to encourage him and Judith obeyed. Judith generally obeyed her aunt; but, though she renounced Bruce Marshall, she would have nothing to do with Eben King or anybody else and all Mrs. Theodora's grumblings did not mend matters.

The afternoon that Mrs. Tony Mack came in Mrs. Theodora felt more aggrieved than ever. Ellie McGregor had been married the previous week—Ellie, who was the same age as Judith and not half so good looking. Mrs. Theodora had been nagging Judith ever since.

"But I might as well talk to the trees down there in that hollow," she complained to Mrs. Tony. "That girl is so set and contrary minded. She doesn't care a bit for my feelings."

This was not said behind Judith's back. The girl herself was standing at the open door, drinking in all the delicate, evasive beauty of the spring afternoon. The Whitney house crested a bare hill that looked down on misty intervals, feathered with young firs that were golden green in the pale sunlight. The fields were bare and smoking, although the lanes and shadowy places were full of moist snow. Judith's face was aglow with the delight of mere life and she bent out to front the brisk, dancing wind that blew up from the valley, resinous with the odors of firs and damp mosses.

At her aunt's words the glow went out of her face. She listened with her eyes brooding on the hollow and a glowing flame of temper smouldering in them. Judith's long patience was giving way. She had been flicked on the raw too often of late. And now her aunt was confiding her grievances to Mrs. Tony Mack—the most notorious gossip in Ramble Valley or out of it!

"I can't sleep at nights for worrying over what will become of her when I'm gone," went on Mrs. Theodora dismally. "She'll just have to live on alone here—a lonesome, withered-up old maid. And her that might have had her pick, Mrs. Tony, though I do say it as shouldn't. You must feel real thankful to have all your girls married off—especially when none of them was extry good-looking. Some people have all the luck. I'm tired of talking to Judith. Folks'll be saying soon that nobody ever really wanted her, for all her flirting. But she just won't marry."

"I will!"

Judith whirled about on the sun warm door step and came in. Her black eyes were flashing and her round cheeks were crimson.

"Such a temper you never saw!" reported Mrs. Tony afterwards. "Though 'tweren't to be wondered at. Theodora was most awful aggravating."

"I will," repeated Judith stormily. "I'm tired of being nagged day in and day out. I'll marry—and what is more I'll marry the very first man that asks me—that I will, if it is old Widower Delane himself! How does that suit you, Aunt Theodora?"

Mrs. Theodora's mental processes were never slow. She dropped her knitting ball and stooped for it. In that time she had decided what to do. She knew that Judith would stick to her word, Stewart-like, and she must trim her sails to catch this new wind.

"It suits me real well, Judith," she said calmly, "you can marry the first man that asks you and I'll say no word to hinder."

The color went out of Judith's face, leaving it pale as ashes. Her hasty assertion had no sooner been uttered than it was repented of, but she must stand by it now. She went out of the kitchen without another glance at her aunt or the delighted Mrs. Tony and dashed up the stairs to her own little room which looked out over the whole of Ramble Valley. It was warm with the March sunshine and the leafless boughs of the creeper that covered the end of the house were tapping a gay tattoo on the window panes to the music of the wind.

Judith sat down in her little rocker and dropped her pointed chin in her hands. Far down the valley, over the firs on the McGregor hill and the blue mirror of the Cranston pond, Bruce Marshall's little gray house peeped out from a semicircle of white-stemmed birches. She had not seen Bruce since before Christmas. He had been angry at her then because she had refused to let him drive her home from prayer meeting. Since then she had heard a rumor that he was going to see Kitty Leigh at the Upper Valley.

Judith looked sombrely down at the Marshall homestead. She had always loved the quaint, picturesque old place, so different from all the commonplace spick and span new houses of the prosperous valley. Judith had never been able to decide whether she really cared very much for Bruce Marshall or not, but she knew that she loved that rambling, cornery house of his, with the gable festooned with the real ivy that Bruce Marshall's great-grandmother had brought with her from England. Judith thought contrastingly of Eben King's staring, primrose-colored house in all its bare, intrusive grandeur. She gave a little shrug of distaste.

"I wish Bruce knew of this," she thought, flushing even in her solitude at the idea. "Although if it is true that he is going to see Kitty Leigh I don't suppose he'd care. And Aunt Theo will be sure to send word to Eben by hook or crook. Whatever possessed me to say such a mad thing? There goes Mrs. Tony now, all agog to spread such a delectable bit of gossip."

Mrs. Tony had indeed gone, refusing Mrs. Theodora's invitation to stay to tea, so eager was she to tell her story. And Mrs. Theodora, at that very minute, was out in her kitchen yard, giving her instructions to Potter Vane, the twelve year old urchin who cut her wood and did sundry other chores for her.

"Potter," she said, excitedly, "run over to the Kings' and tell Eben to come over here immediately—no matter what he's at. Tell him I want to see him about something of the greatest importance."

Mrs. Theodora thought that this was a master stroke.

"That match is as good as made," she thought triumphantly as she picked up chips to start the tea fire. "If Judith suspects that Eben is here she is quite likely to stay in her room and refuse to come down. But if she does I'll march him upstairs to her door and make him ask her through the keyhole. You can't stump Theodora Whitney."

Alas! Ten minutes later Potter returned with the unwelcome news that Eben was away from home.

"He went to Wexbridge about half an hour ago, his ma said. She said she'd tell him to come right over as soon as he kem home."

Mrs. Theodora had to content herself with this, but she felt troubled. She knew Mrs. Tony Mack's capabilities for spreading news. What if Bruce Marshall should hear it before Eben?

That evening Jacob Plowden's store at Wexbridge was full of men, sitting about on kegs and counters or huddling around the stove, for the March air had grown sharp as the sun lowered in the creamy sky over the Ramble Valley hills. Eben King had a keg in the corner. He was in no hurry to go home for he loved gossip dearly and the Wexbridge stores abounded with it. He had exhausted the news of Peter Stanley's store across the bridge and now he meant to hear what was saying at Plowden's. Bruce Marshall was there, too, buying groceries and being waited on by Nora Plowden, who was by no means averse to the service, although as a rule her father's customers received scanty tolerance at her hands.

"What are the Valley roads like, Marshall?" asked a Wexbridge man, between two squirts of tobacco juice.

"Bad," said Bruce briefly. "Another warm day will finish the sleighing."

"Are they crossing at Malley's Creek yet?" asked Plowden.

"No, Jack Carr got in there day before yesterday. Nearly lost his mare. I came round by the main road," responded Bruce.

The door opened at this point and Tony Mack came in. As soon as he closed the door he doubled up in a fit of chuckles, which lasted until he was purple in the face.

"Is the man crazy?" demanded Plowden, who had never seen lean little Tony visited like this before.

"Crazy nothin'," retorted Tony. "You'll laugh too, when you hear it. Such a joke! Hee-tee-tee-hee-e. Theodora Whitney has been badgering Judith Stewart so much about bein' an old maid that Judith's got mad and vowed she'll marry the first man that asks her. Hee-tee-tee-hee-e-e-e! My old woman was there and heard her. She'll keep her word, too. She ain't old Joshua Stewart's daughter for nothin'. If he said he'd do a thing he did it if it tuck the hair off. If I was a young feller now! Hee-tee-tee-hee-e-e-e!"

Bruce Marshall swung round on one foot. His face was crimson and if looks could kill, Tony Mack would have fallen dead in the middle of his sniggers.

"You needn't mind doing up that parcel for me," he said to Nora. "I'll not wait for it."

On his way to the door Eben King brushed past him. A shout of laughter from the assembled men followed them. The others streamed out in their wake, realizing that a race was afoot. Tony alone remained inside, helpless with chuckling.

Eben King's horse was tied at the door. He had nothing to do but step in and drive off. Bruce had put his mare in at Billy Bender's across the bridge, intending to spend the evening there. He knew that this would handicap him seriously, but he strode down the road with a determined expression on his handsome face. Fifteen minutes later he drove past the store, his gray mare going at a sharp gait. The crowd in front of Plowden's cheered him, their sympathies were with him for King was not popular. Tony had come out and shouted, "Here's luck to you, brother," after which he doubled up with renewed laughter. Such a lark! And he, Tony, had set it afoot! It would be a story to tell for years.

Marshall, with his lips set and his dreamy gray eyes for once glittering with a steely light, urged Lady Jane up the Wexbridge hill. From its top it was five miles to Ramble Valley by the main road. A full mile ahead of him he saw Eben King, getting along through mud and slush, and occasional big slumpy drifts of old snow, as fast as his clean-limbed trotter could carry him. As a rule Eben was exceedingly careful of his horses, but now he was sending Bay Billy along for all that was in him.

For a second Bruce hesitated. Then he turned his mare down the field cut to Malley's Creek. It was taking Lady Jane's life and possibly his own in his hand, but it was his only chance. He could never have overtaken Bay Billy on the main road.

"Do your best, Lady Jane," he muttered, and Lady Jane plunged down the steep hillside, through the glutinous mud of a ploughed field as if she meant to do it.

Beyond the field was a ravine full of firs, through which Malley's Creek ran. To cross it meant a four-mile cut to Ramble Valley. The ice looked black and rotten. To the left was the ragged hole where Jack Carr's mare had struggled for her life. Bruce headed Lady Jane higher up. If a crossing could be made at all it was only between Malley's spring-hole and the old ice road. Lady Jane swerved at the bank and whickered.

"On, old girl," said Bruce, in a tense voice. Unwillingly she advanced, picking her steps with cat-like sagacity. Once her foot went through, Bruce pulled her up with hands that did not tremble. The next moment she was scrambling up the opposite bank. Glancing back, Bruce saw the ice parting in her footprints and the black water gurgling up.

But the race was not yet decided. By crossing the creek he had won no more than an equal chance with Eben King. And the field road before him was much worse than the main road. There was little snow on it and some bad sloughs. But Lady Jane was good for it. For once she should not be spared.

Just as the red ball of the sun touched the wooded hills of the valley, Mrs. Theodora, looking from the cowstable door, saw two sleighs approaching, the horses of which were going at a gallop. One was trundling down the main road, headlong through old drifts and slumpy snow, where a false step might send the horse floundering to the bottom. The other was coming up from the direction of the creek, full tilt through Tony Mack's stump land, where not a vestige of snow coated the huge roots over which the runners bumped.

For a moment Mrs. Theodora stood at a gaze. Then she recognized both drivers. She dropped her milking pail and ran to the house, thinking as she ran. She knew that Judith was alone in the kitchen. If Eben King got there first, well and good, but if Bruce Marshall won the race he must encounter her, Mrs. Theodora.

"He won't propose to Judith as long as I'm round," she panted. "I know him—he's too shy. But Eben won't mind—I'll tip him the wink."

Potter Vane was chopping wood before the door. Mrs. Theodora recognizing in him a further obstacle to Marshall's wooing, caught him unceremoniously by the arm and hauled him, axe and all, over the doorstone and into the kitchen, just as Bruce Marshall and Eben King drove into the yard with not a second to spare between them. There was a woeful cut on Bay Billy's slender foreleg and the reeking Lady Jane was trembling like a leaf. The staunch little mare had brought her master over that stretch of sticky field road in time, but she was almost exhausted.

Both men sprang from their sleighs and ran to the door. Bruce Marshall won it by foot-room and burst into the kitchen with his rival hot on his heels. Mrs. Theodora stood defiantly in the middle of the room, still grasping the dazed and dismayed Potter. In a corner Judith turned from the window whence she had been watching the finish of the race. She was pale and tense from excitement. In those few gasping moments she had looked on her heart as on an open book; she knew at last that she loved Bruce Marshall and her eyes met his fiery gray ones as he sprang over the threshold.

"Judith, will you marry me?" gasped Bruce, before Eben, who had first looked at Mrs. Theodora and the squirming Potter, had located the girl.

"Yes," said Judith. She burst into hysterical tears as she said it and sat limply down in a chair.

Mrs. Theodora loosed her grip on Potter.

"You can go back to your work," she said dully. She followed him out and Eben King followed her. On the step she reached behind him and closed the door.

"Trust a King for being too late!" she said bitterly and unjustly.

Eben went home with Bay Billy. Potter gazed after him until Mrs. Theodora ordered him to put Marshall's mare in the stable and rub her down.

"Anyway, Judith won't be an old maid," she comforted herself.

The Promise of Lucy Ellen

Cecily Foster came down the sloping, fir-fringed road from the village at a leisurely pace. Usually she walked with a long, determined stride, but to-day the drowsy, mellowing influence of the Autumn afternoon was strong upon her and filled her with placid content. Without being actively conscious of it, she was satisfied with the existing circumstances of her life. It was half over now. The half of it yet to be lived stretched before her, tranquil, pleasant and uneventful, like the afternoon, filled with unhurried duties and calmly interesting days, Cecily liked the prospect.

When she came to her own lane she paused, folding her hands on the top of the whitewashed gate, while she basked for a moment in the warmth that seemed cupped in the little grassy hollow hedged about with young fir-trees.

Before her lay sere, brooding fields sloping down to a sandy shore, where long foamy ripples were lapping with a murmur that threaded the hushed air like a faint minor melody.

On the crest of the little hill to her right was her home—hers and Lucy Ellen's. The house was an old-fashioned, weather-gray one, low in the eaves, with gables and porches overgrown with vines that had turned to wine-reds and rich bronzes in the October frosts. On three sides it was closed in by tall old spruces, their outer sides bared and grim from long wrestling with the Atlantic winds, but their inner green and feathery. On the fourth side a trim white paling shut in the flower garden before the front door. Cecily could see the beds of purple and scarlet asters, making rich whorls of color under the parlor and sitting-room windows. Lucy Ellen's bed was gayer and larger than Cecily's. Lucy Ellen had always had better luck with flowers.

She could see old Boxer asleep on the front porch step and Lucy Ellen's white cat stretched out on the parlor window-sill. There was no other sign of life about the place. Cecily drew a long, leisurely breath of satisfaction.

"After tea I'll dig up those dahlia roots," she said aloud. "They'd ought to be up. My, how blue and soft that sea is! I never saw such a lovely day. I've been gone longer than I expected. I wonder if Lucy Ellen's been lonesome?"

When Cecily looked back from the misty ocean to the house, she was surprised to see a man coming with a jaunty step down the lane under the gnarled spruces. She looked at him perplexedly. He must be a stranger, for she was sure no man in Oriental walked like that.

"Some agent has been pestering Lucy Ellen, I suppose," she muttered vexedly.

The stranger came on with an airy briskness utterly foreign to Orientalites. Cecily opened the gate and went through. They met under the amber-tinted sugar maple in the heart of the hollow. As he passed, the man lifted his hat and bowed with an ingratiating smile.

He was about forty-five, well, although somewhat loudly dressed, and with an air of self-satisfied prosperity pervading his whole personality. He had a heavy gold watch chain and a large seal ring on the hand that lifted his hat. He was bald, with a high, Shaksperian forehead and a halo of sandy curls. His face was ruddy and weak, but good-natured: his eyes were large and blue, and he had a little straw-colored moustache, with a juvenile twist and curl in it.

Cecily did not recognize him, yet there was something vaguely familiar about him. She walked rapidly up to the house. In the sitting-room she found Lucy Ellen peering out between the muslin window curtains. When the latter turned there was an air of repressed excitement about her.

"Who was that man, Lucy Ellen?" Cecily asked.

To Cecily's amazement, Lucy Ellen blushed—a warm, Spring-like flood of color that rolled over her delicate little face like a miracle of rejuvenescence.

"Didn't you know him? That was Cromwell Biron," she simpered. Although Lucy Ellen was forty and, in most respects, sensible, she could not help simpering upon occasion.

"Cromwell Biron," repeated Cecily, in an emotionless voice. She took off her bonnet mechanically, brushed the dust from its ribbons and bows and went to put it carefully away in its white box in the spare bedroom. She felt as if she had had a severe shock, and she dared not ask anything more just then. Lucy Ellen's blush had frightened her. It seemed to open up dizzying possibilities of change.

"But she promised—she promised," said Cecily fiercely, under her breath.

While Cecily was changing her dress, Lucy Ellen was getting the tea ready in the little kitchen. Now and then she broke out into singing, but always checked herself guiltily. Cecily heard her and set her firm mouth a little firmer.

"If a man had jilted me twenty years ago, I wouldn't be so overwhelmingly glad to see him when he came back—especially if he had got fat and bald-headed," she added, her face involuntarily twitching into a smile. Cecily, in spite of her serious expression and intense way of looking at life, had an irrepressible sense of humor.

Tea that evening was not the pleasant meal it usually was. The two women were wont to talk animatedly to each other, and Cecily had many things to tell Lucy Ellen. She did not tell them. Neither did Lucy Ellen ask any questions, her ill-concealed excitement hanging around her like a festal garment.

Cecily's heart was on fire with alarm and jealousy. She smiled a little cruelly as she buttered and ate her toast.

"And so that was Cromwell Biron," she said with studied carelessness. "I thought there was something familiar about him. When did he come home?"

"He got to Oriental yesterday," fluttered back Lucy Ellen. "He's going to be home for two months. We—we had such an interesting talk this afternoon. He—he's as full of jokes as ever. I wished you'd been here."

This was a fib. Cecily knew it.

"I don't, then," she said contemptuously. "You know I never had much use for Cromwell Biron. I think he had a face of his own to come down here to see you uninvited, after the way he treated you."

Lucy Ellen blushed scorchingly and was miserably silent.

"He's changed terrible in his looks," went on Cecily relentlessly. "How bald he's got—and fat! To think of the spruce Cromwell Biron got to be bald and fat! To be sure, he still has the same sheepish expression. Will you pass me the currant jell, Lucy Ellen?"

"I don't think he's so very fat," she said resentfully, when Cecily had left the table. "And I don't care if he is."

Twenty years before this, Biron had jilted Lucy Ellen Foster. She was the prettiest girl in Oriental then, but the new school teacher over at the Crossways was prettier, with a dash of piquancy, which Lucy Ellen lacked, into the bargain. Cromwell and the school teacher had run away and been married, and Lucy Ellen was left to pick up the tattered shreds of her poor romance as best she could.

She never had another lover. She told herself that she would always be faithful to the one love of her life. This sounded romantic, and she found a certain comfort in it.

She had been brought up by her uncle and aunt. When they died she and her cousin, Cecily Foster, found themselves, except for each other, alone in the world.

Cecily loved Lucy Ellen as a sister. But she believed that Lucy Ellen would yet marry, and her heart sank at the prospect of being left without a soul to love and care for.

It was Lucy Ellen that had first proposed their mutual promise, but Cecily had grasped at it eagerly. The two women, verging on decisive old maidenhood, solemnly promised each other that they would never marry, and would always live together. From that time Cecily's mind had been at ease. In her eyes a promise was a sacred thing.

The next evening at prayer-meeting Cromwell Biron received quite an ovation from old friends and neighbors. Cromwell had been a favorite in his boyhood. He had now the additional glamour of novelty and reputed wealth.

He was beaming and expansive. He went into the choir to help sing. Lucy Ellen sat beside him, and they sang from the same book. Two red spots burned on her thin cheeks, and she had a cluster of lavender chrysanthemums pinned on her jacket. She looked almost girlish, and Cromwell Biron gazed at her with sidelong admiration, while Cecily watched them both fiercely from her pew. She knew that Cromwell Biron had come home, wooing his old love.

"But he sha'n't get her," Cecily whispered into her hymnbook. Somehow it was a comfort to articulate the words, "She promised."

On the church steps Cromwell offered his arm to Lucy Ellen with a flourish. She took it shyly, and they started down the road in the crisp Autumn moonlight. For the first time in ten years Cecily walked home from prayer-meeting alone. She went up-stairs and flung herself on her bed, reckless for once, of her second best hat and gown.

Lucy Ellen did not venture to ask Cromwell in. She was too much in awe of Cecily for that. But she loitered with him at the gate until the grandfather's clock in the hall struck eleven. Then Cromwell went away, whistling gaily, with Lucy Ellen's chrysanthemum in his buttonhole, and Lucy Ellen went in and cried half the night. But Cecily did not cry. She lay savagely awake until morning.

"Cromwell Biron is courting you again," she said bluntly to Lucy Ellen at the breakfast table.

Lucy Ellen blushed nervously.

"Oh, nonsense, Cecily," she protested with a simper.

"It isn't nonsense," said Cecily calmly. "He is. There is no fool like an old fool, and Cromwell Biron never had much sense. The presumption of him!"

Lucy Ellen's hands trembled as she put her teacup down.

"He's not so very old," she said faintly, "and everybody but you likes him—and he's well-to-do. I don't see that there's any presumption."

"Maybe not—if you look at it so. You're very forgiving, Lucy Ellen. You've forgotten how he treated you once."

"No—o—o, I haven't," faltered Lucy Ellen.

"Anyway," said Cecily coldly, "you shouldn't encourage his attentions, Lucy Ellen; you know you couldn't marry him even if he asked you. You promised."

All the fitful color went out of Lucy Ellen's face. Under Cecily's pitiless eyes she wilted and drooped.

"I know," she said deprecatingly, "I haven't forgotten. You are talking nonsense, Cecily. I like to see Cromwell, and he likes to see me because I'm almost the only one of his old set that is left. He feels lonesome in Oriental now."

Lucy Ellen lifted her fawn-colored little head more erectly at the last of her protest. She had saved her self-respect.

In the month that followed Cromwell Biron pressed his suit persistently, unintimidated by Cecily's antagonism. October drifted into November and the chill, drear days came. To Cecily the whole outer world seemed the dismal reflex of her pain-bitten heart. Yet she constantly laughed at herself, too, and her laughter was real if bitter.

One evening she came home late from a neighbor's. Cromwell Biron passed her in the hollow under the bare boughs of the maple that were outlined against the silvery moonlit sky.

When Cecily went into the house, Lucy Ellen opened the parlor door. She was very pale, but her eyes burned in her face and her hands were clasped before her.

"I wish you'd come in here for a few minutes, Cecily," she said feverishly.

Cecily followed silently into the room.

"Cecily," she said faintly, "Cromwell was here to-night. He asked me to marry him. I told him to come to-morrow night for his answer."

She paused and looked imploringly at Cecily. Cecily did not speak. She stood tall and unrelenting by the table. The rigidity of her face and figure smote Lucy Ellen like a blow. She threw out her bleached little hands and spoke with a sudden passion utterly foreign to her.

"Cecily, I want to marry him. I—I—love him. I always have. I never thought of this when I promised. Oh, Cecily, you'll let me off my promise, won't you?"

"No," said Cecily. It was all she said. Lucy Ellen's hands fell to her sides, and the light went out of her face.

"You won't?" she said hopelessly.

Cecily went out. At the door she turned.

"When John Edwards asked me to marry him six years ago, I said no for your sake. To my mind a promise is a promise. But you were always weak and romantic, Lucy Ellen."

Lucy Ellen made no response. She stood limply on the hearth-rug like a faded blossom bitten by frost.

After Cromwell Biron had gone away the next evening, with all his brisk jauntiness shorn from him for the time, Lucy Ellen went up to Cecily's room. She stood for a moment in the narrow doorway, with the lamplight striking upward with a gruesome effect on her wan face.

"I've sent him away," she said lifelessly. "I've kept my promise, Cecily."

There was silence for a moment. Cecily did not know what to say. Suddenly Lucy Ellen burst out bitterly.

"I wish I was dead!"

Then she turned swiftly and ran across the hall to her own room. Cecily gave a little moan of pain. This was her reward for all the love she had lavished on Lucy Ellen.

"Anyway, it is all over," she said, looking dourly into the moonlit boughs of the firs; "Lucy Ellen'll get over it. When Cromwell is gone she'll forget all about him. I'm not going to fret. She promised, and she wanted the promise first."

During the next fortnight tragedy held grim sway in the little weather-gray house among the firs—a tragedy tempered with grim comedy for Cecily, who, amid all her agony, could not help being amused at Lucy Ellen's romantic way of sorrowing.

Lucy Ellen did her mornings' work listlessly and drooped through the afternoons. Cecily would have felt it as a relief if Lucy Ellen had upbraided her, but after her outburst on the night she sent Cromwell away, Lucy Ellen never uttered a word of reproach or complaint.

One evening Cecily made a neighborly call in the village. Cromwell Biron happened to be there and gallantly insisted upon seeing her home.

She understood from Cromwell's unaltered manner that Lucy Ellen had not told him why she had refused him. She felt a sudden admiration for her cousin.

When they reached the house Cromwell halted suddenly in the banner of light that streamed from the sitting-room window. They saw Lucy Ellen sitting alone before the fire, her arms folded on the table, and her head bowed on them. Her white cat sat unnoticed at the table beside her. Cecily gave a gasp of surrender.

"You'd better come in," she said, harshly. "Lucy Ellen looks lonesome."

Cromwell muttered sheepishly, "I'm afraid I wouldn't be company for her. Lucy Ellen doesn't like me much—"

"Oh, doesn't she!" said Cecily, bitterly. "She likes you better than she likes me for all I've—but it's no matter. It's been all my fault—she'll explain. Tell her I said she could. Come in, I say."

She caught the still reluctant Cromwell by the arm and fairly dragged him over the geranium beds and through the front door. She opened the sitting-room door and pushed him in. Lucy Ellen rose in amazement. Over Cromwell's bald head loomed Cecily's dark face, tragic and determined.

"Here's your beau, Lucy Ellen," she said, "and I give you back your promise."

She shut the door upon the sudden illumination of Lucy Ellen's face and went up-stairs with the tears rolling down her cheeks.

"It's my turn to wish I was dead," she muttered. Then she laughed hysterically.

"That goose of a Cromwell! How queer he did look standing there, frightened to death of Lucy Ellen. Poor little Lucy Ellen! Well, I hope he'll be good to her."

The Pursuit of the Ideal

Freda's snuggery was aglow with the rose-red splendour of an open fire which was triumphantly warding off the stealthy approaches of the dull grey autumn twilight. Roger St. Clair stretched himself out luxuriously in an easy-chair with a sigh of pleasure.

"Freda, your armchairs are the most comfy in the world. How do you get them to fit into a fellow's kinks so splendidly?"

Freda smiled at him out of big, owlish eyes that were the same tint as the coppery grey sea upon which the north window of the snuggery looked.

"Any armchair will fit a lazy fellow's kinks," she said.

"I'm not lazy," protested Roger. "That you should say so, Freda, when I have wheeled all the way out of town this dismal afternoon over the worst bicycle road in three kingdoms to see you, bonnie maid!"

"I like lazy people," said Freda softly, tilting her spoon on a cup of chocolate with a slender brown hand.

Roger smiled at her chummily.

"You are such a comfortable girl," he said. "I like to talk to you and tell you things."

"You have something to tell me today. It has been fairly sticking out of your eyes ever since you came. Now, 'fess."

Freda put away her cup and saucer, got up, and stood by the fireplace, with one arm outstretched along the quaintly carved old mantel. She laid her head down on its curve and looked expectantly at Roger.

"I have seen my ideal, Freda," said Roger gravely.

Freda lifted her head and then laid it down again. She did not speak. Roger was glad of it. Even at the moment he found himself thinking that Freda had a genius for silence. Any other girl he knew would have broken in at once with surprised exclamations and questions and spoiled his story.

"You have not forgotten what my ideal woman is like?" he said.

Freda shook her head. She was not likely to forget. She remembered only too keenly the afternoon he had told her. They had been sitting in the snuggery, herself in the inglenook, and Roger coiled up in his big pet chair that nobody else ever sat in.

"'What must my lady be that I must love her?'" he had quoted. "Well, I will paint my dream-love for you, Freda. She must be tall and slender, with chestnut hair of wonderful gloss, with just the suggestion of a ripple in it. She must have an oval face, colourless ivory in hue, with the expression of a Madonna; and her eyes must be 'passionless, peaceful blue,' deep and tender as a twilight sky."

Freda, looking at herself along her arm in the mirror, recalled this description and smiled faintly. She was short and plump, with a piquant, irregular little face, vivid tinting, curly, unmanageable hair of ruddy brown, and big grey eyes. Certainly, she was not his ideal.

"When and where did you meet your lady of the Madonna face and twilight eyes?" she asked.

Roger frowned. Freda's face was solemn enough but her eyes looked as if she might be laughing at him.

"I haven't met her yet. I have only seen her. It was in the park yesterday. She was in a carriage with the Mandersons. So beautiful, Freda! Our eyes met as she drove past and I realized that I had found my long-sought ideal. I rushed back to town and hunted up Pete Manderson at the club. Pete is a donkey but he has his ways of being useful. He told me who she was. Her name is Stephanie Gardiner; she is his cousin from the south and is visiting his mother. And, Freda, I am to dine at the Mandersons' tonight. I shall meet her."

"Do goddesses and ideals and Madonnas eat?" said Freda in an awed whisper. Her eyes were certainly laughing now. Roger got up stiffly.

"I must confess I did not expect that you would ridicule my confidence, Freda," he said frigidly. "It is very unlike you. But if you are not interested I will not bore you with any further details. And it is time I was getting back to town anyhow."

When he had gone Freda ran to the west window and flung it open. She leaned out and waved both hands at him over the spruce hedge.

"Roger, Roger, I was a horrid little beast. Forget it immediately, please. And come out tomorrow and tell me all about her."

Roger came. He bored Freda terribly with his raptures but she never betrayed it. She was all sympathy—or, at least, as much sympathy as a woman can be who must listen while the man of men sings another woman's praises to her. She sent Roger away in perfect good hu-humour with himself and all the world, then she curled herself up in the snuggery, pulled a rug over her head, and cried.

Roger came out to Lowlands oftener than ever after that. He had to talk to somebody about Stephanie Gardiner and Freda was the safest vent. The "pursuit of the Ideal," as she called it, went on with vim and fervour. Sometimes Roger would be on the heights of hope and elation; the next visit he would be in the depths of despair and humility. Freda had learned to tell which it was by the way he opened the snuggery door.

One day when Roger came he found six feet of young man reposing at ease in his particular chair. Freda was sipping chocolate in her corner and looking over the rim of her cup at the intruder just as she had been wont to look at Roger. She had on a new dark red gown and looked vivid and rose-hued.

She introduced the stranger as Mr. Grayson and called him Tim. They seemed to be excellent friends. Roger sat bolt upright on the edge of a fragile, gilded chair which Freda kept to hide a shabby spot in the carpet, and glared at Tim until the latter said goodbye and lounged out.

"You'll be over tomorrow?" said Freda.

"Can't I come this evening?" he pleaded.

Freda nodded. "Yes—and we'll make taffy. You used to make such delicious stuff, Tim."

"Who is that fellow, Freda?" Roger inquired crossly, as soon as the door closed.

Freda began to make a fresh pot of chocolate. She smiled dreamily as if thinking of something pleasant.

"Why, that was Tim Grayson—dear old Tim. He used to live next door to us when we were children. And we were such chums—always together, making mud pies, and getting into scrapes. He is just the same old Tim, and is home from the west for a long visit. I was so glad to see him again."

"So it would appear," said Roger grumpily. "Well, now that 'dear old Tim' is gone, I suppose I can have my own chair, can I? And do give me some chocolate. I didn't know you made taffy."

"Oh, I don't. It's Tim. He can do everything. He used to make it long ago, and I washed up after him and helped him eat it. How is the pursuit of the Ideal coming on, Roger-boy?"

Roger did not feel as if he wanted to talk about the Ideal. He noticed how vivid Freda's smile was and how lovable were the curves of her neck where the dusky curls were caught up from it. He had also an inner vision of Freda making taffy with Tim and he did not approve of it.

He refused to talk about the Ideal. On his way back to town he found himself thinking that Freda had the most charming, glad little laugh of any girl he knew. He suddenly remembered that he had never heard the Ideal laugh. She smiled placidly—he had raved to Freda about that smile—but she did not laugh. Roger began to wonder what an ideal without any sense of humour would be like when translated into the real.

He went to Lowlands the next afternoon and found Tim there—in his chair again. He detested the fellow but he could not deny that he was good-looking and had charming manners. Freda was very nice to Tim. On his way back to town Roger decided that Tim was in love with Freda. He was furious at the idea. The presumption of the man!

He also remembered that he had not said a word to Freda about the Ideal. And he never did say much more—perhaps because he could not get the chance. Tim was always there before him and generally outstayed him.

One day when he went out he did not find Freda at home. Her aunt told him that she was out riding with Mr. Grayson. On his way back he met them. As they cantered by, Freda waved her riding whip at him. Her face was full of warm, ripe, kissable tints, her loose lovelocks were blowing about it, and her eyes shone like grey pools mirroring stars. Roger turned and watched them out of sight behind the firs that cupped Lowlands.

That night at Mrs. Crandall's dinner table somebody began to talk about Freda. Roger strained his ears to listen. Mrs. Kitty Carr was speaking—Mrs. Kitty knew everything and everybody.

"She is simply the most charming girl in the world when you get really acquainted with her," said Mrs. Kitty, with the air of having discovered and patented Freda. "She is so vivid and unconventional and lovable—'spirit and fire and dew,' you know. Tim Grayson is a very lucky fellow."

"Are they engaged?" someone asked.

"Not yet, I fancy. But of course it is only a question of time. Tim simply adores her. He is a good soul and has lots of money, so he'll do. But really, you know, I think a prince wouldn't be good enough for Freda."

Roger suddenly became conscious that the Ideal was asking him a question of which he had not heard a word. He apologized and was forgiven. But he went home a very miserable man.

He did not go to Lowlands for two weeks. They were the longest, most wretched two weeks he had ever lived through. One afternoon he heard that Tim Grayson had gone back west. Mrs. Kitty told it mournfully.

"Of course, this means that Freda has refused him," she said. "She is such an odd girl."

Roger went straight out to Lowlands. He found Freda in the snuggery and held out his hands to her.

"Freda, will you marry me? It will take a lifetime to tell you how much I love you."

"But the Ideal?" questioned Freda.

"I have just discovered what my ideal is," said Roger. "She is a dear, loyal, companionable little girl, with the jolliest laugh and the warmest, truest heart in the world. She has starry grey eyes, two dimples, and a mouth I must and will kiss—there—there—there! Freda, tell me you love me a little bit, although I've been such a besotted idiot."

"I will not let you call my husband-that-is-to-be names," said Freda, snuggling down into the curve of his shoulder. "But indeed, Roger-boy, you will have to make me very, very happy to square matters up. You have made me so unutterably unhappy for two months."

"The pursuit of the Ideal is ended," declared Roger.

The Softening of Miss Cynthia

"I wonder if I'd better flavour this cake with lemon or vanilla. It's the most perplexing thing I ever heard of in my life."

Miss Cynthia put down the bottles with a vexed frown; her perplexity had nothing whatever to do with flavouring the golden mixture in her cake bowl. Mrs. John Joe knew that; the latter had dropped in in a flurry of curiosity concerning the little boy whom she had seen about Miss Cynthia's place for the last two days. Her daughter Kitty was with her; they both sat close together on the kitchen sofa.

"It *is* too bad," said Mrs. John Joe sympathetically. "I don't wonder you are mixed up. So unexpected, too! When did he come?"

"Tuesday night," said Miss Cynthia. She had decided on the vanilla and was whipping it briskly in. "I saw an express wagon drive into the yard with a boy and a trunk in it and I went out just as he got down. 'Are you my Aunt Cynthia?' he said. 'Who in the world are you?' I asked. And he says, 'I'm Wilbur Merrivale, and my father was John Merrivale. He died three weeks ago and he said I was to come to you, because you were his sister.' Well, you could just have knocked me down with a feather!"

"I'm sure," said Mrs. John Joe. "But I didn't know you had a brother. And his name—Merrivale?"

"Well, he wasn't any relation really. I was about six years old when my father married his mother, the Widow Merrivale. John was just my age, and we were brought up together just like brother and sister. He was a real nice fellow, I must say. But he went out to Californy years ago, and I haven't heard a word of him for fifteen years—didn't know if he was alive or dead. But it seems from what I can make out from the boy, that his mother died when he was a baby, and him and John roughed it along together—pretty poor, too, I guess—till John took a fever and died. And he told some of his friends to send the boy to me, for he'd no relations there and not a cent in the world. And the child came all the way from Californy, and here he is. I've been just distracted ever since. I've never been used to children, and to have the house kept in perpetual uproar is more than I can stand. He's about twelve and a born mischief. He'll tear through the rooms with his dirty feet, and he's smashed one of my blue vases and torn down a curtain and set Towser on the cat half a dozen times already—I never was so worried. I've got him out on the verandah shelling peas now, to keep him quiet for a little spell."

"I'm really sorry for you," said Mrs. John Joe. "But, poor child, I suppose he's never had anyone to look after him. And come all the way from Californy alone, too—he must be real smart."

"Too smart, I guess. He must take after his mother, whoever she was, for there ain't a bit of Merrivale in him. And he's been brought up pretty rough."

"Well, it'll be a great responsibility for you, Cynthia, of course. But he'll be company, too, and he'll be real handy to run errands and—"

"*I'm* not going to keep him," said Miss Cynthia determinedly. Her thin lips set themselves firmly and her voice had a hard ring.

"Not going to keep him?" said Mrs. John Joe blankly. "You can't send him back to Californy!"

"I don't intend to. But as for having him here to worry my life out and keep me in a perpetual stew, I just won't do it. D'ye think I'm going to trouble myself about children at my age? And all he'd cost for clothes and schooling, too! I can't afford it. I don't suppose his father expected it either. I suppose he expected me to look after him a bit—and of course I will. A boy of his age ought to be able to earn his keep, anyway. If I look out a place for him somewhere where he can do odd jobs and go to school in the winter, I think it's all anyone can expect of me, when he ain't really no blood relation."

Miss Cynthia flung the last sentence at Mrs. John Joe rather defiantly, not liking the expression on that lady's face.

"I suppose nobody could expect more, Cynthy," said Mrs. John Joe deprecatingly. "He would be an awful bother, I've no doubt, and you've lived alone so long with no one to worry you that you wouldn't know what to do with him. Boys are always getting into mischief—my four just keep me on the dead jump. Still, it's a pity for him, poor little fellow! No mother or father—it seems hard."

Miss Cynthia's face grew grimmer than ever as she went to the door with her callers and watched them down the garden path. As soon as

Mrs. John Joe saw that the door was shut, she unburdened her mind to her daughter.

"Did you ever hear tell of the like? I thought I knew Cynthia Henderson well, if anybody in Wilmot did, but this beats me. Just think, Kitty—there she is, no one knows how rich, and not a soul in the world belonging to her, and she won't even take in her brother's child. She must be a hard woman. But it's just meanness, pure and simple; she grudges him what he'd eat and wear. The poor mite doesn't look as if he'd need much. Cynthia didn't used to be like that, but it's growing on her every day. She's got hard as rocks."

That afternoon Miss Cynthia harnessed her fat grey pony into the phaeton herself—she kept neither man nor maid, but lived in her big, immaculate house in solitary state—and drove away down the dusty, buttercup-bordered road, leaving Wilbur sitting on the verandah. She returned in an hour's time and drove into the yard, shutting the gate behind her with a vigorous snap. Wilbur was not in sight and, fearful lest he should be in mischief, she hurriedly tied the pony to the railing and went in search of him. She found him sitting by the well, his chin in his hands; he was pale and his eyes were red. Miss Cynthia hardened her heart and took him into the house.

"I've been down to see Mr. Robins this afternoon, Wilbur," she said, pretending to brush some invisible dust from the bottom of her nice black cashmere skirt for an excuse to avoid looking at him, "and he's agreed to take you on trial. It's a real good chance—better than you could expect. He says he'll board and clothe you and let you go to school in the winter."

The boy seemed to shrink.

"Daddy said that I would stay with you," he said wistfully. "He said you were so good and kind and would love me for his sake."

For a moment Miss Cynthia softened. She had been very fond of her stepbrother; it seemed that his voice appealed to her across the grave in behalf of his child. But the crust of years was not to be so easily broken.

"Your father meant that I would look after you," she said, "and I mean to, but I can't afford to keep you here. You'll have a good place at Mr. Robins', if you behave yourself. I'm going to take you down now, before I unharness the pony, so go and wash your face while I put up your things. Don't look so woebegone, for pity's sake! I'm not taking you to prison."

Wilbur turned and went silently to the kitchen. Miss Cynthia thought she heard a sob. She went with a firm step into the little bedroom off the hall and took a purse out of a drawer.

"I s'pose I ought," she said doubtfully. "I don't s'pose he has a cent. I daresay he'll lose or waste it."

She counted out seventy-five cents carefully. When she came out, Wilbur was at the door. She put the money awkwardly into his hand.

"There, see that you don't spend it on any foolishness."

Miss Cynthia's Action made a good deal of talk in Wilmot. The women, headed by Mrs. John Joe—who said behind Cynthia's back what she did not dare say to her face—condemned her. The men laughed and said that Cynthia was a shrewd one; there was no getting round her. Miss Cynthia herself was far from easy. She could not forget Wilbur's wistful eyes, and she had heard that Robins was a hard master.

A week after the boy had gone she saw him one day at the store. He was lifting heavy bags from a cart. The work was beyond his strength, and he was flushed and panting. Miss Cynthia's conscience gave her a hard stab. She bought a roll of peppermints and took them over to him. He thanked her timidly and drove quickly away.

"Robins hasn't any business putting such work on a child," she said to herself indignantly. "I'll speak to him about it."

And she did—and got an answer that made her ears tingle. Mr. Robins bluntly told her he guessed he knew what was what about his hands. He weren't no nigger driver. If she wasn't satisfied, she might take the boy away as soon as she liked.

Miss Cynthia did not get much comfort out of life that summer. Almost everywhere she went she was sure to meet Wilbur, engaged in some hard task. She could not help seeing how miserably pale and thin he had become. The worry had its effect on her. The neighbours said that Cynthy was sharper than ever. Even her church-going was embittered. She had always enjoyed walking up the aisle with her rich silk skirt rustling over the carpet, her cashmere shawl folded correctly over her shoulders, and her lace bonnet set precisely on her thin shining crimps. But she could take no pleasure in that or in the sermon now, when Wilbur sat right across from her pew, between hard-featured Robins and his sulky-looking wife. The boy's eyes had grown too large for his thin face.

The softening of Miss Cynthia was a very gradual process, but it reached a climax one September morning, when Mrs. John Joe came into the former's kitchen with an important face. Miss Cynthia was preserving her plums.

"No, thank you, I'll not sit down—I only run in—I suppose you've heard it. That little Merrivale boy has took awful sick with fever, they say. He's been worked half to death this summer—everyone knows what Robins is with his help—and they say he has fretted a good deal for his father and been homesick, and he's run down, I s'pose. Anyway, Robins took him over to the hospital at Stanford last night—good gracious, Cynthy, are you sick?"

Miss Cynthia had staggered to a seat by the table; her face was pallid.

"No, it's only your news gave me a turn—it came so suddenly—I didn't know."

"I must hurry back and see to the men's dinners. I thought I'd come and tell you, though I didn't know as you'd care."

This parting shot was unheeded by Miss Cynthia. She laid her face in her hands. "It's a judgement on me," she moaned. "He's going to die, and I'm his murderess. This is the account I'll have to give John Merrivale of his boy. I've been a wicked, selfish woman, and I'm justly punished."

It was a humbled Miss Cynthia who met the doctor at the hospital that afternoon. He shook his head at her eager questions.

"It's a pretty bad case. The boy seems run down every way. No, it is impossible to think of moving him again. Bringing him here last night did him a great deal of harm. Yes, you may see him, but he will not know you, I fear—he is delirious and raves of his father and California."

Miss Cynthia followed the doctor down the long ward. When he paused by a cot, she pushed past him. Wilbur lay tossing restlessly on his pillow. He was thin to emaciation, but his cheeks were crimson and his eyes burning bright.

Miss Cynthia stooped and took the hot, dry hands in hers.

"Wilbur," she sobbed, "don't you know me—Aunt Cynthia?"

"You are not my Aunt Cynthia," said Wilbur. "Daddy said Aunt Cynthia was good and kind—you are a cross, bad woman. I want Daddy. Why doesn't he come? Why doesn't he come to little Wilbur?"

Miss Cynthia got up and faced the doctor.

"He's *got* to get better," she said stubbornly. "Spare no expense or trouble. If he dies, I will be a murderess. He must live and give me a chance to make it up for him."

And he did live; but for a long time it was a hard fight, and there were days when it seemed that death must win. Miss Cynthia got so thin and wan that even Mrs. John Joe pitied her.

The earth seemed to Miss Cynthia to laugh out in prodigal joyousness on the afternoon she drove home when Wilbur had been pronounced out of danger. How tranquil the hills looked, with warm October sunshine sleeping on their sides and faint blue hazes on their brows! How gallantly the maples flaunted their crimson flags! How kind and friendly was every face she met! Afterwards, Miss Cynthia said she began to live that day.

Wilbur's recovery was slow. Every day Miss Cynthia drove over with some dainty, and her loving gentleness sat none the less gracefully on her because of its newness. Wilbur grew to look for and welcome her coming. When it was thought safe to remove him, Miss Cynthia went to the hospital with a phaeton-load of shawls and pillows.

"I have come to take you away," she said.

Wilbur shrank back. "Not to Mr. Robins," he said piteously. "Oh, not there, Aunt Cynthia!"

Them Notorious Pigs

John Harrington was a woman-hater, or thought that he was, which amounts to the same thing. He was forty-five and, having been handsome in his youth, was a fine-looking man still. He had a remarkably good farm and was a remarkably good farmer. He also had a garden which was the pride and delight of his heart or, at least, it was before Mrs. Hayden's pigs got into it.

Sarah King, Harrington's aunt and housekeeper, was deaf and crabbed, and very few visitors ever came to the house. This suited Harrington. He was a good citizen and did his duty by the community, but his bump of sociability was undeveloped. He was also a contented man, looking after his farm, improving his stock, and experimenting with new bulbs in undisturbed serenity. This, however, was all too good to last. A man is bound to have some troubles in this life, and Harrington's were near their beginning when Perry Hayden bought the adjoining farm from the heirs of Shakespeare Ely, deceased, and moved in.

To be sure, Perry Hayden, poor fellow, did not bother Harrington much, for he died of pneumonia a month after he came there, but his widow carried on the farm with the assistance of a lank hired boy. Her own children, Charles and Theodore, commonly known as Bobbles and Ted, were as yet little more than babies.

The real trouble began when Mary Hayden's pigs, fourteen in number and of half-grown voracity, got into Harrington's garden. A railing, a fir grove, and an apple orchard separated the two establishments, but these failed to keep the pigs within bounds.

Harrington had just got his garden planted for the season, and to go out one morning and find a horde of enterprising porkers rooting about in it was, to put it mildly, trying. He was angry, but as it was a first offence he drove the pigs out with tolerable calmness, mended the fence, and spent the rest of the day repairing damages.

Three days later the pigs got in again. Harrington relieved his mind by some scathing reflections on women who tried to run farms. Then he sent Mordecai, his hired man, over to the Hayden place to ask Mrs. Hayden if she would be kind enough to keep her pigs out of his garden. Mrs. Hayden sent back word that she was very sorry and would not let it occur again. Nobody, not even John Harrington, could doubt that she meant what she said. But she had reckoned without the pigs. They had not forgotten the flavour of Egyptian fleshpots as represented by the succulent young shoots in the Harrington domains. A week later Mordecai came in and told Harrington that "them notorious pigs" were in his garden again.

There is a limit to everyone's patience. Harrington left Mordecai to drive them out, while he put on his hat and stalked over to the Haydens' place. Ted and Bobbles were playing at marbles in the lane and ran when they saw him coming. He got close up to the little low house among the apple trees before Mordecai appeared in the yard, driving the pigs around the barn. Mrs. Hayden was sitting on her doorstep, paring her dinner potatoes, and stood up hastily when she saw her visitor.

Harrington had never seen his neighbour at close quarters before. Now he could not help seeing that she was a very pretty little woman, with wistful, dark blue eyes and an appealing expression. Mary Hayden had been next to a beauty in her girlhood, and she had a good deal of her bloom left yet, although hard work and worry were doing their best to rob her of it. But John Harrington was an angry man and did not care whether the woman in question was pretty or not. Her pigs had rooted up his garden—that fact filled his mind.

"Mrs. Hayden, those pigs of yours have been in my garden again. I simply can't put up with this any longer. Why in the name of reason don't you look after your animals better? If I find them in again I'll set my dog on them, I give you fair warning."

A faint colour had crept into Mary Hayden's soft, milky-white cheeks during this tirade, and her voice trembled as she said, "I'm very sorry, Mr. Harrington. I suppose Bobbles forgot to shut the gate of their pen again this morning. He is so forgetful."

"I'd lengthen his memory, then, if I were you," returned Harrington grimly, supposing that Bobbles was the hired man. "I'm not going to have my garden ruined just because he happens to be forgetful. I am speaking my mind plainly, madam. If you can't keep your stock from being a nuisance to other people you ought not to try to run a farm at all."

Then did Mrs. Hayden sit down upon the doorstep and burst into tears. Harrington felt, as Sarah King would have expressed it, "every which way at once." Here was a nice mess! What a nuisance women were—worse than the pigs!

"Oh, don't cry, Mrs. Hayden," he said awkwardly. "I didn't mean—well, I suppose I spoke too strongly. Of course I know you didn't mean to let the pigs in. There, do stop crying! I beg your pardon if I've hurt your feelings."

"Oh, it isn't that," sobbed Mrs. Hayden, wiping away her tears. "It's only—I've tried so hard—and everything seems to go wrong. I make such mistakes. As for your garden, sir. I'll pay for the damage my pigs have done if you'll let me know what it comes to."

She sobbed again and caught her breath like a grieved child. Harrington felt like a brute. He had a queer notion that if he put his arm around her and told her not to worry over things women were not created to attend to he would be expressing his feelings better than in any other way. But of course he couldn't do that. Instead, he muttered that the damage didn't amount to much after all, and he hoped she wouldn't mind what he said, and then he got himself away and strode through the orchard like a man in a desperate hurry.

Mordecai had gone home and the pigs were not to be seen, but a chubby little face peeped at him from between two scrub, bloom-white cherry trees.

"G'way, you bad man!" said Bobbles vindictively. "G'way! You made my mommer cry—I saw you. I'm only Bobbles now, but when I grow up I'll be Charles Henry Hayden and you won't dare to make my mommer cry then."

Harrington smiled grimly. "So you're the lad who forgets to shut the pigpen gate, are you? Come out here and let me see you. Who is in there with you?"

"Ted is. He's littler than me. But I won't come out. I don't like you. G'way home."

Harrington obeyed. He went home and to work in his garden. But work as hard as he would, he could not forget Mary Hayden's grieved face.

"I was a brute!" he thought. "Why couldn't I have mentioned the matter gently? I daresay she has enough to trouble her. Confound those pigs!"

After that there was a time of calm. Evidently something had been done to Bobbles' memory or perhaps Mrs. Hayden attended to the gate herself. At all events the pigs were not seen and Harrington's garden blossomed like the rose. But Harrington himself was in a bad state.

For one thing, wherever he looked he saw the mental picture of his neighbour's tired, sweet face and the tears in her blue eyes. The original he never saw, which only made matters worse. He wondered what opinion she had of him and decided that she must think him a cross old bear. This worried him. He wished the pigs would break in again so that he might have a chance to show how forbearing he could be.

One day he gathered a nice mess of tender young greens and sent them over to Mrs. Hayden by Mordecai. At first he had thought of sending her some flowers, but that seemed silly, and besides, Mordecai and flowers were incongruous. Mrs. Hayden sent back a very pretty message of thanks, whereat Harrington looked radiant and Mordecai, who could see through a stone wall as well as most people, went out to the barn and chuckled.

"Ef the little widder hain't caught him! Who'd a-thought it?"

The next day one adventurous pig found its way alone into the Harrington garden. Harrington saw it get in and at the same moment he saw Mrs. Hayden running through her orchard. She was in his yard by the time he got out.

Her sunbonnet had fallen back and some loose tendrils of her auburn hair were curling around her forehead. Her cheeks were so pink and her eyes so bright from running that she looked almost girlish.

"Oh, Mr. Harrington," she said breathlessly, "that pet pig of Bobbles' is in your garden again. He only got in this minute. I saw him coming and I ran right after him."

"He's there, all right," said Harrington cheerfully, "but I'll get him out in a jiffy. Don't tire yourself. Won't you go into the house and rest while I drive him around?"

Mrs. Hayden, however, was determined to help and they both went around to the garden, set the gate open, and tried to drive the pig out. But Harrington was not thinking about pigs, and Mrs. Hayden did not know quite so much about driving them as Mordecai did; as a consequence they did not make much headway. In her excitement Mrs. Hayden ran over beds and whatever came in her way, and Harrington, in order to keep near her, ran after her. Between them they spoiled things about as much as a whole drove of pigs would have done.

But at last the pig grew tired of the fun, bolted out of the gate, and ran across the yard to his own place. Mrs. Hayden followed slowly and Harrington walked beside her.

"Those pigs are all to be shut up tomorrow," she said. "Hiram has been fixing up a place for them in his spare moments and it is ready at last."

"Oh, I wouldn't," said Harrington hastily. "It isn't good for pigs to be shut up so young. You'd better let them run a while yet."

"No," said Mrs. Hayden decidedly. "They have almost worried me to death already. In they go tomorrow."

They were at the lane gate now, and Harrington had to open it and let her pass through. He felt quite desperate as he watched her trip up through the rows of apple trees, her blue gingham skirt brushing the lush grasses where a lacy tangle of sunbeams and shadows lay. Bobbles and Ted came running to meet her and the three, hand in hand, disappeared from sight.

Harrington went back to the house, feeling that life was flat, stale, and unprofitable. That evening at the tea table he caught himself wondering what it would be like to see Mary Hayden sitting at his table in place of Sarah King, with Bobbles and Ted on either hand. Then he found out what was the matter with him. He was in love, fathoms deep, with the blue-eyed widow!

Presumably the pigs were shut up the next day, for Harrington's garden was invaded no more. He stood it for a week and then surrendered at discretion. He filled a basket with early strawberries and went across to the Hayden place, boldly enough to all appearance, but with his heart thumping like any schoolboy's.

The front door stood hospitably open, flanked by rows of defiant red and yellow hollyhocks. Harrington paused on the step, with his hand outstretched to knock. Somewhere inside he heard a low sobbing. Forgetting all about knocking, he stepped softly in and walked to the door of the little sitting-room. Bobbles was standing behind him in the middle of the kitchen but Harrington did not see him. He was looking at Mary Hayden, who was sitting by the table in the room with her arms flung out over it and her head bowed on them. She was crying softly in a hopeless fashion.

Harrington put down his strawberries. "Mary!" he exclaimed.

Mrs. Hayden straightened herself up with a start and looked at him, her lips quivering and her eyes full of tears.

"What is the matter?" said Harrington anxiously. "Is anything wrong?"

"Oh, nothing much," Said Mrs. Hayden, trying to recover herself. "Yes, there is too. But it is very foolish of me to be going on like this. I didn't know anyone was near. And I was feeling so discouraged. The colt broke his leg in the swamp pasture today and Hiram had to shoot him. It was Ted's colt. But there, there is no use in crying over it."

And by way of proving this, the poor, tired, overburdened little woman began to cry again. She was past caring whether Harrington saw her or not.

The woman-hater was so distressed that he forgot to be nervous. He sat down and put his arm around her and spoke out what was in his mind without further parley.

"Don't cry, Mary. Listen to me. You were never meant to run a farm and be killed with worry. You ought to be looked after and petted. I want you to marry me and then everything will be all right. I've loved you ever since that day I came over here and made you cry. Do you think you can like me a little, Mary?"

It may be that Mrs. Hayden was not very much surprised, because Harrington's face had been like an open book the day they chased the pig out of the garden together. As for what she said, perhaps Bobbles, who was surreptitiously gorging himself on Harrington's strawberries, may tell you, but I certainly shall not.

The little brown house among the apple trees is shut up now and the boundary fence belongs to ancient history. Sarah King has gone also and Mrs. John Harrington reigns royally in her place. Bobbles and Ted have a small, blue-eyed, much-spoiled sister, and there is a pig on the estate who may die of old age, but will never meet his doom otherwise. It is Bobbles' pig and one of the famous fourteen.

Mordecai still shambles around and worships Mrs. Harrington. The garden is the same as of yore, but the house is a different place and Harrington is a different man. And Mordecai will tell you with a chuckle, "It was them notorious pigs as did it all."

Why Not Ask Miss Price?

Frances Allen came in from the post office and laid an open letter on the table beside her mother, who was making mincemeat. Alma Allen looked up from the cake she was frosting to ask, "What is the matter? You look as if your letter contained unwelcome news, Fan."

"So it does. It is from Aunt Clara, to say she cannot come. She has received a telegram that her sister-in-law is very ill and she must go to her at once."

Mrs. Allen looked regretful, and Alma cast her spoon away with a tragic air.

"That is too bad. I feel as if our celebration were spoiled. But I suppose it can't be helped."

"No," agreed Frances, sitting down and beginning to peel apples. "So there is no use in lamenting, or I would certainly sit down and cry, I feel so disappointed."

"Is Uncle Frank coming?"

"Yes, Aunt Clara says he will come down from Stellarton if Mrs. King does not get worse. So that will leave just one vacant place. We must invite someone to fill it up. Who shall it be?"

Both girls looked rather puzzled. Mrs. Allen smiled a quiet little smile all to herself and went on chopping suet. She had handed the Thanksgiving dinner over to Frances and Alma this year. They were to attend to all the preparations and invite all the guests. But although they had made or planned several innovations in the dinner itself, they had made no change in the usual list of guests.

"It must just be the time-honoured family affair," Frances had declared. "If we begin inviting other folks, there is no knowing when to draw the line. We can't have more than fourteen, and some of our friends would be sure to feel slighted."

So the same old list it was. But now Aunt Clara—dear, jolly Aunt Clara, whom everybody in the connection loved and admired—could not come, and her place must be filled.

"We can't invite the new minister, because we would have to have his sister, too," said Frances. "And there is no reason for asking any one of our girl chums more than another."

"Mother, you will have to help us out," said Alma. "Can't you suggest a substitute guest?"

Mrs. Allen looked down at the two bright, girlish faces turned up to her and said slowly, "I think I can, but I am not sure my choice will please you. Why not ask Miss Price?"

Miss Price! They had never thought of her! She was the pale, timid-looking little teacher in the primary department of the Hazelwood school.

"Miss Price?" repeated Frances slowly. "Why, Mother, we hardly know her. She is dreadfully dull and quiet, I think."

"And so shy," said Alma. "Why, at the Wards' party the other night she looked startled to death if anyone spoke to her. I believe she would be frightened to come here for Thanksgiving."

"She is a very lonely little creature," said Mrs. Allen gently, "and doesn't seem to have anyone belonging to her. I think she would be very glad to get an invitation to spend Thanksgiving elsewhere than in that cheerless little boarding-house where she lives."

"Of course, if you would like to have her, Mother, we will ask her," said Frances.

"No, girls," said Mrs. Allen seriously. "You must not ask Miss Price on my account, if you do not feel prepared to make her welcome for her own sake. I had hoped that your own kind hearts might have prompted you to extend a little Thanksgiving cheer in a truly Thanksgiving spirit to a lonely, hard-working girl whose life I do not think is a happy one. But there, I shall not preach. This is your dinner, and you must please yourselves as to your guests."

Frances and Alma had both flushed, and they now remained silent for a few minutes. Then Frances sprang up and threw her arms around her mother.

"You're right, Mother dear, as you always are, and we are very selfish girls. We will ask Miss Price and try to give her a nice time. I'll go down this very evening and see her."

In the grey twilight of the chilly autumn evening Bertha Price walked home to her boarding-house, her pale little face paler, and her grey eyes sadder than ever, in the fading light. Only two days until

Thanksgiving—but there would be no real Thanksgiving for her. Why, she asked herself rebelliously, when there seemed so much love in the world, was she denied her share?

Her landlady met her in the hall.

"Miss Allen is in the parlour, Miss Price. She wants to see you."

Bertha went into the parlour somewhat reluctantly. She had met Frances Allen only once or twice and she was secretly almost afraid of the handsome, vivacious girl who was so different from herself.

"I am sorry you have had to wait, Miss Allen," she said shyly. "I went to see a pupil of mine who is ill and I was kept later than I expected."

"My errand won't take very long," said Frances brightly. "Mother wants you to spend Thanksgiving Day with us, Miss Price, if you have no other engagement. We will have a few other guests, but nobody outside our own family except Mr. Seeley, who is the law partner and intimate friend of my brother Ernest in town. You'll come, won't you?"

"Oh, thank you, yes," said Bertha, in pleased surprise. "I shall be very glad to go. Why, it is so nice to think of it. I expected my Thanksgiving Day to be lonely and sad—not a bit Thanksgivingy."

"We shall expect you then," said Frances, with a cordial little handsqueeze. "Come early in the morning, and we will have a real friendly, pleasant day."

That night Frances said to her mother and sister, "You never saw such a transfigured face as Miss Price's when I asked her up. She looked positively pretty—such a lovely pink came out on her cheeks and her eyes shone like stars. She reminded me so much of somebody I've seen, but I can't think who it is. I'm so glad we've asked her here for Thanksgiving!"

Thanksgiving came, as bright and beautiful as a day could be, and the Allens' guests came with it. Bertha Price was among them, paler and shyer than ever. Ernest Allen and his friend, Maxwell Seeley, came out from town on the morning train.

After all the necessary introductions had been made, Frances flew to the kitchen.

"I've found out who it is Miss Price reminds me of," she said, as she bustled about the range. "It's Max Seeley. You needn't laugh, Al. It's a fact. I noticed it the minute I introduced them. He's plump and prosperous and she's pinched and pale, but there's a resemblance nevertheless. Look for yourself and see if it isn't so."

Back in the big, cheery parlour the Thanksgiving guests were amusing themselves in various ways. Max Seeley had given an odd little start when he was introduced to Miss Price, and as soon as possible he followed her to the corner where she had taken refuge. Ernest Allen was out in the kitchen talking to his sisters, the "uncles and cousins and aunts" were all chattering to each other, and Mr. Seeley and Miss Price were quite unnoticed.

"You will excuse me, won't you, Miss Price, if I ask you something about yourself?" he said eagerly. "The truth is, you look so strikingly like someone I used to know that I feel sure you must be related to her. I do not think I have any relatives of your name. Have you any of mine?"

Bertha flushed, hesitated for an instant, then said frankly, "No, I do not think so. But I may as well tell you that Price is not my real name and I do not know what it is, although I think it begins with S. I believe that my parents died when I was about three years old, and I was then taken to an orphan asylum. The next year I was taken from there and adopted by Mrs. Price. She was very kind to me and treated me as her own daughter. I had a happy home with her, although we were poor. Mrs. Price wished me to bear her name, and I did so. She never told me my true surname, perhaps she did not know it. She died when I was sixteen, and since then I have been quite alone in the world. That is all I know about myself."

Max Seeley was plainly excited.

"Why do you think your real name begins with S?" he asked.

"I have a watch which belonged to my mother, with the monogram 'B.S.' on the case. It was left with the matron of the asylum and she gave it to Mrs. Price for me. Here it is."

Max Seeley almost snatched the old-fashioned little silver watch, from her hand and opened the case. An exclamation escaped him as he pointed to some scratches on the inner side. They looked like the initials M.A.S.

"Let me tell my story now," he said. "My name is Maxwell Seeley. My father died when I was seven years old, and my mother a year later. My little sister, Bertha, then three years old, and I were left quite alone and very poor. We had no relatives. I was adopted by a well-to-do old bachelor, who had known my father. My sister was taken to an orphan asylum in a city some distance away. I was very much attached to her and grieved bitterly over our parting. My adopted father was very kind to me and gave me a good education. I did not forget my sister, and as soon as I could I went to the asylum. I found that she had been taken away long before, and I could not even discover who had adopted her, for the original building, with all its records, had been destroyed by fire two years previous to my visit. I never could find any clue to her whereabouts, and long since gave up all hope of finding her. But I have found her at last. You are Bertha Seeley, my little sister!"

"Oh—can it be possible!"

"More than possible—it is certain. You are the image of my mother, as I remember her, and as an old daguerreotype I have pictures her. And this is her watch—see, I scratched my own initials on the case one day. There is no doubt in the world. Oh, Bertha, are you half as glad as I am?"

"Glad!"

Bertha's eyes were shining like stars. She tried to smile, but burst into tears instead and her head went down on her brother's shoulder. By this time everybody in the room was staring at the extraordinary tableau, and Ernest, coming through the hall, gave a whistle of astonishment that brought the two in the corner back to a sense of their surroundings.

"I haven't suddenly gone crazy, Ernest, old fellow," smiled Max. "Ladies and gentlemen all, this little school-ma'am was introduced to you as Miss Price, but that was a mistake. Let me introduce her again as Miss Bertha Seeley, my long-lost and newly-found sister."

Well they had an amazing time then, of course. They laughed and questioned and explained until the dinner was in imminent danger of getting stone-cold on the dining-room table. Luckily, Alma and Frances remembered it just in the nick of time, and they all got out, somehow, and into their places. It was a splendid dinner, but I believe that Maxwell and Bertha Seeley didn't know what they were eating, any more than if it had been sawdust. However, the rest of the guests made up for that, and did full justice to the girls' cookery.

In the afternoon they all went to church, and at least two hearts were truly and devoutly thankful that day.

When the dusk came, Ernest and Maxwell had to catch the last train for town, and the other guests went home, with the exception of Bertha, who was to stay all night. Just as soon as her resignation could be effected, she was to join her brother.

"Meanwhile, I'll see about getting a house to put you in," said Max. "No more boarding out for me, Ernest. You may consider me as a family man henceforth."

Frances and Alma talked it all over before they went to sleep that night.

"Just think," said Frances, "if we hadn't asked her here today she might never have found her brother! It's all Mother's doing, bless her! Things do happen like a storybook sometimes, don't they, Al? And didn't I tell you they looked alike?"

The Buln-Buln and the Brolga
Joseph Furphy
Benediction Classics, 2011
94 pages
ISBN: 978-1-84902-416-7

Available from www.amazon.com, www.amazon.co.uk

The Buln-Buln and the Brolga is a long story, written by Joseph Furphy in 1905. This book is a study of Fred, the liar, set off by Bob, the Bush-yarner who is also prone to exaggeration. It challenges to look at the vagaries of marriage, death, deceit and the embarrassing dehumanisation of the native people. Written by the author of "Such is Life", and indeed the story started off as a discarded chapter in the novel, it deals with similar issues, most significantly the individual's perception of reality, sometimes with humour and parody.

Gomez Arias;
Or The Moors Of The Alpujarras.
A Spanish Historical Romance
Joaquín Telesforo De Trueba Y Cosío
Benediction Classics, 2011
354 pages
ISBN: 978-1-84902-462-4

Available from www.amazon.com, www.amazon.co.uk

This paperback includes all three Volumes of the novel 'Gomez Arias The Moors of the Alpujarras, A Spanish Historical Romance'. It was written in 1826 by the Spaniard Joaquín Telesforo de Trueba y Cosío who wrote in English and belonged to the Romantic movement. It is set in the province of Granada. A censored version was produced in 1831

Crestlands - A Centennial Story of Cane Ridge - with illustrations
Mary Addams Bayne
Benediction Classics, 2011
228 pages
ISBN: 978-1-84902-325-2

Available from www.amazon.com, www.amazon.co.uk

Crestlands, A Centennial Story of Cane Ridge is a romance, set in Kentucky during the early part of the nineteenth century. The story gives a fascinating portrayal of the life and conditions for the people at this time. The book comes complete with original illustrations.

Famous Novels -(unabridged) Lost Horizon, Knight Without Armour, Goodbye, Mr. Chips, Random Harvest, The Story of Dr Wassell, & So Well Remembered
James Hilton
Oxford City Press, 2012
830 pages
ISBN: 978-1-78139-202-7

Available from www.amazon.com, www.amazon.co.uk

James Hilton was an eminent novelist, many of his stories critiquing English culture. His first novel was published when he was just 20, and several of his books were international best sellers and successfully adapted for film. This is a compilation brings together Hilton's most famous novels, all unabridged: Lost Horizon, Knight Without Armour , Goodbye, Mr. Chips, Random Harvest, The Story of Dr Wassell and So Well Remembered.

Also from Benediction Books ...

Wandering Between Two Worlds: Essays on Faith and Art
Anita Mathias
Benediction Books, 2007
152 pages
ISBN: 0955373700

Available from www.amazon.com, www.amazon.co.uk

In these wide-ranging lyrical essays, Anita Mathias writes, in lush, lovely prose, of her naughty Catholic childhood in Jamshedpur, India; her large, eccentric family in Mangalore, a sea-coast town converted by the Portuguese in the sixteenth century; her rebellion and atheism as a teenager in her Himalayan boarding school, run by German missionary nuns, St. Mary's Convent, Nainital; and her abrupt religious conversion after which she entered Mother Teresa's convent in Calcutta as a novice. Later rich, elegant essays explore the dualities of her life as a writer, mother, and Christian in the United States-- Domesticity and Art, Writing and Prayer, and the experience of being "an alien and stranger" as an immigrant in America, sensing the need for roots.

About the Author

Anita Mathias is the author of *Wandering Between Two Worlds: Essays on Faith and Art*. She has a B.A. and M.A. in English from Somerville College, Oxford University, and an M.A. in Creative Writing from the Ohio State University, USA. Anita won a National Endowment of the Arts fellowship in Creative Nonfiction in 1997. She lives in Oxford, England with her husband, Roy, and her daughters, Zoe and Irene.

Anita's website:
http://www.anitamathias.com, and
Anita's blog Dreaming Beneath the Spires:
http://dreamingbeneaththespires.blogspot.com

The Church That Had Too Much
Anita Mathias
Benediction Books, 2010
52 pages
ISBN: 9781849026567

Available from www.amazon.com, www.amazon.co.uk

The Church That Had Too Much was very well-intentioned. She wanted to love God, she wanted to love people, but she was both hampered by her muchness and the abundance of her possessions, and beset by ambition, power struggles and snobbery. Read about the surprising way The Church That Had Too Much began to resolve her problems in this deceptively simple and enchanting fable.

About the Author

Anita Mathias is the author of *Wandering Between Two Worlds: Essays on Faith and Art*. She has a B.A. and M.A. in English from Somerville College, Oxford University, and an M.A. in Creative Writing from the Ohio State University, USA. Anita won a National Endowment of the Arts fellowship in Creative Nonfiction in 1997. She lives in Oxford, England with her husband, Roy, and her daughters, Zoe and Irene.

Anita's website:
http://www.anitamathias.com, and
Anita's blog Dreaming Beneath the Spires:
http://dreamingbeneaththespires.blogspot.com

www.ingramcontent.com/pod-product-compliance
Lightning Source LLC
Chambersburg PA
CBHW030344310726
48979CB00001B/175
* 9 7 8 1 7 8 1 3 9 2 4 1 6 *